SPARKS FROM THE FIRE

Sparks from
the Fire

by

Rosalie Parker

Swan River Press
Dublin, Ireland
MMXXIV

Sparks from the Fire
by Rosalie Parker

Published by
Swan River Press
at Æon House
Dublin, Ireland
June MMXXIV

www.swanriverpress.ie
brian@swanriverpress.ie

Cover design by Meggan Kehrli
from artwork by R. B. Russell

Set in Garamond by Ken Mackenzie

Paperback Edition
ISBN 978-1-78380-776-5

Swan River Press published
a limited hardback edition of
Sparks from the Fire in June 2018.

Contents

To Ray and Tim,
for everything

The Bronze Statuette

Hannah held the bronze statuette up to the light. It was small, fitting easily in her hand. She was pretty sure that it was the likeness of a classical god, and it was a fairly standard representation, except for the eyes, the whites of which had been inlaid with ivory, while the pupils were little chips of verdigrised bronze. This had a disconcerting effect, making the figure more lifelike and, perhaps because of this, more peculiar. If genuine, it was a remarkable survival.

"Yes, I'll buy it," she said to the olive-skinned young man who had brought the statuette into the shop. "How much do you want for it? It's rather small."

"Aren't you going to ask me where I found it?"

She laughed, "Yes of course. It was your granny's."

"I found it on a grave in Highgate Cemetery, but now I don't want it any more. You can have it for fifty pounds."

"Okay. Fifty it is." Hannah opened the till and removed two twenties and a ten. The young man stared at her. "Don't you want the money then?"

He pocketed the notes. "It was just standing on a grave, and I thought it was interesting so I took it. I couldn't read the name on the gravestone, it had eroded away."

"You shouldn't be telling me this."

"It was just as you see it now. No dirt or grime. As clean as a whistle. So I took it home."

Hannah idly picked up a reference book from below the counter and began scanning the index.

"I hoped it would bring me luck, but I don't want it anymore."

"So you said. It's mine now, anyway."

"That's right." His smile transformed his face. He seemed almost relieved.

"Well off you go then. If you 'find' any more antiquities you know where I am."

When he had gone she opened her laptop. After half an hour of browsing, her research was inconclusive, but if she had to hazard a guess, she'd say from the scanty evidence that the statuette represented a minor deity called Phthonus, a Greek god. He wasn't exactly beautiful, but he was a novelty, and novelty always sold. She wrote out a label and, after a moment's thought, added a price of £650. Opening up the counter display case, she positioned the little god in front of the Roman coins and Egyptian grave goods so that he stared out into the shop, where he might attract the attention of some of her better off customers.

That evening Hannah made herself scrambled eggs and opened a bottle of wine. Sphinx, her cat, lovingly rubbed around her legs while she cooked. After her meal she looked again at the new artefacts she had brought up the stairs to her flat. The little bronze statuette was easily the most intriguing—under a magnifying glass his naked form was revealed as beautifully modelled and the eyes were really alarming. He had a slight squint and as well as being forever awake, peering not quite at you but off to one side. They reminded Hannah of those staring eye masks you could buy in joke shops. Further research on the internet had not shaken her belief that he was Phthonus, god of envy who, it seemed, specialised in matters pertaining to sexual jealousy. He was the go-between who had informed Hera of Zeus's many infidelities. A bit of a sneak, then. Those eyes, she thought, would see everything: every nuance, every lustful glance, every intrigue, every small betrayal . . .

The telephone rang.

"Hi Hannah. Sorry I didn't phone last night."

"That's okay. Were you at work?"

"Yes, well . . . kind of. We took Sherman out for a meal. He's thinking of investing so it called for some serious schmoozing."

"And is it working?"

"It's hard to tell. He hasn't come across yet."

"Are you hung over, Mark, or do you want to come round?"

"Er, I'm okay. A bit tired. Perhaps we could leave it until tomorrow."

"I bought a strange little god today."

"You bought a what?"

"He's a bit special. I'll show you tomorrow."

The next morning Hannah was dusting a fifteenth-century carving of an angel when Sam Bright walked into the shop. Sam was a general antique dealer who owned an upmarket shop in the West End.

"I've just popped in to see how the competition's doing."

He ran his finger along the counter display case. "My, you have some fabulous stuff in, darling." He pointed at the little god. "Where on earth did you find him?"

"One of my regulars brought him in. A metal detector find, I think."

"Don't you *know*? . . . tut tut. Can I have a look?"

Hannah unlocked the cabinet and handed the statuette to Sam.

"Oh those horrid eyes! Greek, isn't he? Gorgeous! Can I buy him?" He looked at the label, "Ouch! Not for anything like that much, you naughty girl."

"I think I'm going to keep hold of him, Sam. Someone will pay that for him, you know they will."

"Spoil sport." He put the god back in the display case. "Sell me some of your Egyptian tat, then."

Hannah let him have three of the less commercial pieces at a reasonable dealers' discount. As he paid, he leaned over, his peppermint breath full in her face. "Just remember, Hannah love, you've only been here five minutes. Some of us have years of experience."

"What do you want me to do about it, Sam, pack up and go home? Where would you find your stock then?"

Of the seven customers that came in the shop that morning, five commented on the statuette and three asked for a closer look. One woman shivered theatrically. "He's quite ghastly, isn't he?" she said. "I don't think I'd want him in the house." Hannah explained about the attribution to Phthonus, but the woman, who was looking for a birthday present for her husband, unsurprisingly, decided that he was unsuitable. Hannah talked her into buying a small earthenware Anubis instead. Later, an elderly man in tweeds asked for a magnifying glass and took Phthonus to the window so that he could examine him in better light. He looked at Hannah thoughtfully.

"You may be right about the attribution; I don't know for sure. I imagine he would've been placed in a household shrine, perhaps as a warning to an errant wife or husband? An unusual subject." But he didn't buy him. The little god resumed his place at the front of the display cabinet.

The Waggon and Horses was crowded at lunchtime, and Hannah had to eat her sandwiches with the smokers outside. She took out her mobile phone and tried Mark's number, but he was not answering. Hannah had brought the statuette with her. She retrieved him from her bag, stood him on the table and began taking photographs for her website. This drew some attention from her fellow diners.

"Crikey!" said the man sitting at the next table, "are you looking at my bird?"

His companion shrieked with laughter. Hannah put Phthonus back in her bag.

Mark reclined decorously on her sofa. Phthonus stood on the coffee table.

Mark called out to Hannah in the kitchen, "Is this your strange little god?" He picked him up. "He's seriously freaky, isn't he? Don't you want to keep him?"

Hannah came in with two glasses of wine. She handed one to Mark. "I don't think so. He's pretty rare, but I'm not sure I like the way he looks at my customers."

Mark laughed. "He does have a bit of squint."

Hannah sighed, "Yes, but it's more than that. He's smug. It's like he knows something."

"What on earth do you mean?" Mark laughed.

Hannah was well aware that, even after explaining about Phthonus's role in the Greek pantheon, her feelings about the statuette weren't entirely rational.

The bronze statuette had failed to sell. There had been plenty of interest, and Hannah was willing to drop the asking price, but she was aware that her heart wasn't in it. She suspected that her ambivalence about the strange little god had communicated itself to the customers.

Phthonus was out on the counter when the door opened and Sam Bright came in.

"Ah hah!" he said, homing in on the little god. "You haven't sold this naughty chap! He looks a bit cross, doesn't he! Are you ready to sell him to me? I've a customer for him if you will."

A spark of pride made Hannah answer, "No can do, Sam. Sorry. It's only been two weeks."

Sam's brick-red face paled dramatically. "Well, thank you, Hannah. I thought after all the free advice I've given you, you might be a little more grateful . . . "

"I seem to remember that you advised me to open a dress shop. Frankly, Sam, you've inveigled quite a lot of my stock into your shop, and you're still showing every sign of *wanting* me to fail. Well, bad luck because I'm not going to. Anyway, you're the one with the swanky address and clientele to match. How can I be a threat to you?"

Sam, showing more dignity than she thought he possessed, gathered himself and stalked out, leaving Hannah kicking herself that over the statuette she had probably lost her best trade customer.

The party was extravagant, with seemingly limitless bottles of real champagne, caviar, and canapés. Hannah was carefully dressed in her little black number, and had put her hair up in a loose bun. Mark steered Hannah towards a short, middle-aged man standing in the corner.

"Hannah, this is Terry Sherman. Terry is a good client of ours. Perhaps I could just leave you two to chat for a couple of minutes?"

And Mark somehow disappeared, leaving Hannah struggling with the monosyllabic Sherman. Sherman livened up, however, when she told him about her shop.

"Oh, how quaint," he warbled. "Do people still open real shops?"

Hannah spotted Mark talking to a dark-haired woman on the other side of the room, his head bent to hers, the space between them negligible. Sherman topped up Hannah's champagne glass and was talking about his investment portfolio, but she had stopped listening. The woman was young and wore a daringly low-cut green dress. Sherman, noticing Hannah's inattention, put his hand on her arm. At that moment Mark looked up. He frowned, then stalked over.

"Hands off, Sherman," he said.

"I-I beg your pardon!"

"You heard. She's mine." And with that Mark took Hannah's arm and steered her towards the canapés.

"Wow," she said. "He wasn't doing anything he shouldn't have. He's just a bore. Who were you talking to?"

"Oh, no-one."

"Well, she was *someone.*"

"She's Sherman's daughter, Marie. I have to butter these people up. It's my job."

"Well you've just blown it with Sherman, haven't you?"

"He'll probably forget about it. I don't know what came over me really."

Hannah reached up and kissed him.

"What's that for?"

"Don't you know?"

Hannah added the photographs of the little bronze god to her website, lowering the price to £550. She had acquired several good American customers with a taste for more unusual items, and there was every chance that one of them would be interested.

The shop bell rang and the olive skinned young man walked in.

"Hello," she said, hastily covering the bronze statuette and its price tag with the *London Evening News*, "have you brought me something interesting?"

"I haven't brought you anything. I've come to take back the little god. You paid me fifty pounds." He held out a handful of notes.

"No, no, no," she laughed, "it doesn't work like that. He's mine now and I fully intend to sell him for a profit."

"I think it's fair that you sell him back to me. I took him, which was not fair. And I want to put him back."

"What do you mean, put him back?"

"I want to put him back on the grave where I found him. In Highgate Cemetery. Then he will lose his power."

"Lose his *power*? He's not Superman."

"He will lose his power to make me unhappy. I have been imagining such horrible things . . ."

Hannah closed her eyes. "Look, I'm not selling him back to you—do you understand?"

The young man sighed. "Then you are unkind as well as dishonest. You are rich and I am poor . . ."

"I'm *not* rich . . ."

"I think, relatively speaking, you are. You have a shop. I am a student. I cannot really afford to pay you fifty pounds, but I must." He was close to tears. He held out the money.

Hannah laughed uneasily. "Look, this is daft. I really can't help you, and I'm going to have to ask you to leave."

He was openly crying now. "My girlfriend, Nadia, has left me. Please help me."

"I'm sorry, but if you won't leave I will call the police."

He shuffled towards the door. "I believe you have no heart at all."

Hannah barely had time to make a cup of tea before Terry Sherman and Marie walked in.

"Hello," said Sherman, "we thought we'd take a look at your little shop. I so enjoyed listening to you talk about it at the party. Mark told us where to find you."

Hannah removed the newspaper from the counter display case. "It was great talking to you. I hope you didn't mind Mark . . ."

Terry laughed in a rather forced way. "Not at all. No worries. I can see why he feels protective . . . "

Marie smirked. She was a good looking girl of about eighteen, with glossy brown hair and bright clothes. "Mark thought we might like some of your *weirder* merchandise," she drawled. "He said something about a strange little god?"

Hannah took Phthonus out of the case and handed him to Marie. "Perhaps an acquired taste, but he's extremely rare and unusual . . . "

Marie guffawed rudely. "He's a total minger! Oh dad, we're not buying him just so you can get in her knickers, are we?"

Terry cringed, "*Marie . . .* "

"Oh please! Let's buy some of this pretty Egyptian stuff instead."

Feeling like the hired help, Hannah found the presence of mind to pick out five of her more expensive Egyptian pieces, which Sherman was embarrassed enough to pay for and take away.

Afterwards, neither Hannah nor Mark could remember exactly why the row started. She was telling him about the events in the shop and Marie was mentioned. Mark shifted uncomfortably in his seat.

"It's not easy," he said. I don't really fancy her, but I have to be nice to her because of her dad. You do understand, don't you?"

"You don't *really* fancy her?"

"Oh for God's sake! Look, she plays up to it. She knows the score."

"Oh poor you! It's bad enough having to put up with Sherman pawing me, let alone his daughter flaunting herself . . . "

"Well, what about Sherman? He fancies the pants off you . . . and he's absolutely loaded!"

And so it continued, even after they'd been to bed, shopped, and had dinner. They'd never had a row over anything so ridiculous before.

The next day Hannah phoned Sam Bright and offered to sell him the bronze statuette for £500. He, obviously enjoying himself, beat down the price to £400. He came over in the afternoon to collect it.

"No hard feelings, Hannah. It's a fair price. Between you and me, the buyer I have in mind is Greek, so this little fellow will be going home, won't he?" Sam patted the god's unmoving hair. Hannah wrapped him up in tissue paper and bubblewrap, then handed him over.

"How much will your Greek pay for him?"

"Now, now, you know I'm paying you a decent price. I could ask how much *you* paid for him!"

As Sam left, Hannah felt a great surge of relief.

Hannah and Mark had agreed to a sort of trial separation, even though they didn't live together—Mark had a flat in Kilburn. In fact, it had been Mark who suggested it. With Phthonus out of the way, Hannah hoped things would settle down and they could begin seeing each other again.

The headline blazed out of the front page of the day's *London Evening News*: Hannah recognised the photo of the olive skinned young man at once:

Woman Stabs Jealous Boyfriend

Sociology student, Said Karemi, 21, is in intensive care tonight after a row with his ex-girlfriend led to serious knife injuries. Friends of the injured man named the perpetrator as Nadia Boutros, 20, who is now believed to be in police custody. Peter Davis, 21, friend of the couple said, "I think she just snapped. Said had become extremely possessive and jealous of Nadia, which led her to end the relationship. But he didn't seem to be able to move on. It's so sad, they were a lovely couple. None of us really knows what went wrong."

Mr. Karemi has undergone emergency surgery and is expected to survive his injuries.

It was absurd, she thought, to blame a god of dubious provenance for this, but surely Karemi was unaware of the attribution of the deity . . . ? He didn't know anything about him, but had simply found the god on a grave. Hopefully Karemi would recover from his wounds, but she dreaded the possibility that he might make another visit to her shop. She shuddered, glad that Phthonus was no longer her responsibility. Now that he had gone, Hannah expected that she and Mark would be able to stop their ridiculous bickering. She was confident that she could persuade him to leave Marie alone and come and live with her above the shop, where she would be able to keep a much closer eye on him. And they would be happy, beyond the gaze of the bronze statuette . . .

The Fell Race

Several days had passed since the incident, and the villagers were still coming to terms with the fact that their young people would have to lie low for a while. Mike's two teenage daughters were caught up in it and he informed them that they would be grounded for the next month. This was, he liked to think, more for their own protection than for any other reason—it was not a punishment. Many parents had taken the same course of action, although there were a few who were more inclined to leniency, whether through choice or laziness he didn't know. The real fear of many in the village was that the local newspaper would get to hear of the incident, resulting in some sort of a garbled version of events being cobbled into a story which would be at best only half the truth. And half the truth would be bad enough if it got out to the wider world.

Not that everything could be swept under the carpet. The air ambulance had rescued two of the more seriously injured runners—both had broken legs and were still in hospital. So far, though, the police had not become involved. The injuries had been put down to unlucky accidents. It seemed to be tacitly understood in the village that for the sake of all concerned this was how things should stay.

There had never been a similar occurrence—the under-eighteen fell race had been run at every village event since anyone could remember. The small silver trophies presented to the boy and girl winners were worn smooth with polishing, the route up to and down from the fell similarly eroded by the feet of the racers, the more serious of whom trained for the event for some weeks beforehand. A significant cash prize for the winner and runners up had helped ensure a healthy number of participants over the years.

Mike's daughters Chloë and Charlotte had never been grounded before, and were spending much of their time keeping in touch with the other fell runners on social media. Charlotte was trying to find out if anyone had taken photographs, but it seemed that everyone had been wearing racing strip without pockets and had left their mobile phones behind. There was a great deal of sympathy for those who had been injured, but no one had yet admitted seeing exactly how the injuries had occurred.

Charlotte sat up on her bed. "I don't see why we should be punished for something we can't even remember. There could be any number of reasons for what happened. Maybe there was gas escaping from the old lead mines or something and we all blacked out."

"I remember some of the race, don't you?" said Chloë. "Slogging up the fields on to the moor, being overtaken by just about everyone else. You were ahead of me. Then the cloud came down and it was difficult to see more than a few metres ahead. The shouts came from somewhere near the top, then I lost track and I can't remember anything else until the rescue party found us wandering about in the heather. None of it makes much sense."

They had reprised the story several times.

"I know," said Charlotte. "It's the same for everyone, more or less."

"We've come out of it reasonably well. Maggie Dawson is really upset and is taking diazepam. Several people are badly cut and bruised. Joe and Sarah are still in hospital and will be in plaster for several months."

Mike had been searching the internet for similar incidents, but found little that seemed to fit. There was a mass hallucination during a village celebration in Mexico, but that was thought to have a religious cause. Several disappearances during long-distance races were reported, although he felt disinclined to believe in them. He probably would not have believed what happened at the fell race if his own daughters had not been involved. It seemed to him that there was more they could tell him if they wanted to. A whole field of competitors could not simply have become lost on a hillside that was well known to them.

Charlotte and Chloë soon grew tired of their incarceration. Not that there was much to do in the village in the evenings, but they missed the youth club meetings and dances in the nearby town, and badminton in the neighbouring village.

"Thank heavens for Facebook," said Chloë.

"This is daft, though," said Charlotte. "What do they think they're protecting us from? We're going to school every day."

"I suppose they're worried about something they don't understand."

"Well, we don't understand it either, but keeping us in our rooms isn't going to make any difference. So what if it gets in the papers, it's old news now, anyway."

Joe and Sarah had been released from hospital, but neither could remember much about how they had come by their broken legs. Both had joined the Facebook debate. It was noticeable to the young people that their parents were reluctant to lift the curfew. Exams were looming and it was almost as if the incident was being used as an excuse to keep them in their rooms revising. Mike, for one, was prepared to admit that he found it more comfortable when he knew his daughters were safe in their bedrooms.

But the time came when the curfew had to be lifted and the teenagers of the village were free to meet up once more. Mike drove Charlotte and Chloë to the youth club dance.

"It feels like ages since we were allowed out," said Charlotte.

Most of the other fell runners were there. They sat in the chairs around the dance floor.

"I don't feel like dancing," said Chloë. "It doesn't feel right when Joe and Sarah can hardly walk."

The runners huddled together and talked only of the incident, and why they were unable to remember what had happened. Some of the parents seemed to believe there had been some kind of fight caused by over-competitiveness, but no-one who was actually there could remember anything of the kind. However, as they could recall little, nothing could be ruled out. That was part of the problem.

While the girls were at the youth club, Mike met his friend John in the village pub. John's son Ian had been one of those most affected by whatever had happened on the fell.

"He's just not the same," said John. "He's much more lifeless somehow. He's gone to youth club, but his heart's not in it."

Mike nodded. "I don't know what my two are thinking. They've stopped talking to me about anything important. I almost wish they had boyfriends. It might take them out of themselves."

"None of them seem to be dating. Maybe it's delayed shock."

"Do you think we ought to get them some counselling?" asked Mike.

"I don't know. You hear some funny stories about that sort of thing. Do we really want to stir it up even more?"

At the youth club each fell runner was taking it in turns to relate, yet again, what they remembered about the incident. Maggie Dawson was already in tears.

"I was doing really well, and hoping I might win. You couldn't see much through the cloud but I know the fell so well it didn't matter. Sarah was right in front of me and I was shaping up to pass her when I heard a shout ahead. Then I remember nothing until the rescue party found us. I can't stop thinking about it. How on earth did Joe and Sarah end up with broken legs?"

"I can't help wondering whether there might be more to it," said Chloë. "Something must've happened in the time we lost up there. But what? It can only have been half an hour before the rescue party arrived."

"Wouldn't it be worse if nothing happened?" asked Ian. "If we just slipped through time. But why us? That's what I want to know."

The discussion meandered around on the same track for the rest of the evening, as it had on Facebook during the weeks the curfew had been in place.

The youth club dance was the last event that any of the runners attended before their exams. All of the teenagers in the village stayed in their rooms revising or sending messages to each other. Mike, John, and the other parents had now become concerned about their children's apparent loss of confidence in social situations, but could hardly insist that they should go out when the exams where so close. Mike had been visiting websites dealing with teenage anxiety, but the girls did not seem particularly anxious, or at least he thought not, although it was difficult to tell when they were hardly talking to him.

The summer wore on and the exams came and went. Chloë and Charlotte had been expected to do well but at the last parents' evening their teachers were more down-beat, asking if there was anything wrong at home. The teenagers of the village were still keeping mostly to their rooms and it seemed there was little their parents could do to entice them out. Many of the older teenagers, including Chloë, had applied to various universities earlier in the year and were waiting for their exam results to see if they had been accepted.

The parents began meeting regularly in the pub to discuss their children. Although the physical wounds had mostly healed, it seemed that the fell runners were unable to move on from the trauma of the race. Mike did not subscribe to the theory that there had been some kind of fight. He felt, as did John, that the most likely explanation was that the runners had been party to a mass hallucination brought on by disorientation after the sudden descent of the cloud. A vote was taken on the counselling issue and it was agreed that the fell runners should be carefully looked after, with parents watching out for any more worrying behaviour. It was generally felt that time would be the best healer. The jury was out as to whether or not the next fell race would go ahead at the church fete at the beginning of September. Mike was against it.

Chloë and Charlotte had found a chat site dedicated to strange happenings—UFO sightings, out-of-body experiences, remote viewing, etc. Ian had taken up evangelical Christianity in a big way. Maggie was into yoga and mindfulness. All over the village, paths to enlightenment and understanding were being explored.

Two days before the first exam results were due, Chloë and Charlotte disappeared from their rooms. At first Mike thought the girls had simply gone out to meet friends. He was relieved that they had at last seen fit to leave the house of their own accord. But when they failed to return for dinner he rang round their friends' parents and discovered that many of the teenagers were missing.

The parents met at the pub to decide whether or not to call the police. When half the village turned up it was clear that they were going to have to involve the authorities. It seemed that every one of the fell runners was missing, including Joe and Sarah, who were still on crutches.

"We should've done something about this before," said Susan Dawson. "We all knew there was something wrong. How could we have let it come to this?"

Mike shrugged, "They might be somewhere close by—they'll have arranged to meet via Facebook. There may be nothing to worry about. We've all been wanting them to go out more, after all. Chloë and Charlotte haven't packed bags or taken their laptops. Perhaps they'll be back before it gets dark."

There was a gloomy silence. John said, "I'll phone the police."

The other parents nodded.

Above the village, on the fell, the low cloud descended once more. Only the mournful warble of the curlew disturbed the silence. Already, small stones and plants were encroaching onto the unused route of the fell race, reclaiming the edges of the scar. Soon bilberry, grass, and heather would regenerate on the bare peaty earth at the centre of the track.

View from a Window

My friends raved about the view from my study. Tristram said, "How lucky you are! I could look at it forever." He often returned to the window to watch the changes that mark the progress of each day: the gradual greening of the grass, light moving over the fields, a larger flock of crows. Amanda said, "He has fallen in love. I can't compete with the beauty of it." She laughed, but I could see that she felt excluded, for although she admired the view, she did not share Tristram's wild enthusiasm.

Amanda and Tristram have gone back to London and I am working hard to make up for the days I spent driving them around. We went to the loch, the town and the distillery: the rest of the time they were happy to sit in the back of the car and absorb the scenery. They came to offer moral support, but their stay soon turned into a holiday. As they boarded the train to go home Amanda embraced me and said they'd had a lovely time. "And look after yourself," she added, almost as an afterthought.

I am working in my study and steel myself to look at the view; the mountain, the burn and the unfurling fronds of bracken. It's like my own face, solemn and familiar, the green clothing the rock like flesh over bone. I have lived here for eight years and thought I would never tire of it, but life moves on and love is spoilt when you least expect it. Tristram said he could look at the view forever, but if a genie granted his wish, he'd never be able to leave the study. He'd be trapped in there for ever, his nose pressed to the glass.

Some days I try to feel about the view the way I used to, but I can't conjure up the old emotions.

It's been raining for what seems like weeks. The last fine days were in April. This morning there is an easterly wind which belies the time of year. The burn rages down the mountainside and tumbles into the swollen river. Everything is wet. I have already given up on the garden—the slugs in any case have destroyed the seedlings I planted in the spring. It's a mass of damp perennials, shaggy grass and weeds and will probably stay that way until the house is sold.

I'm writing a script for a radio play. My editor has been very kind, but I know he fears it will not be finished in time. It's about a homeless girl and her progress through the city. The girl suffers many tribulations, but it ends happily. It's very worthy, but that's what my editor wants. I have learnt to be an honest critic of my work, and to stick to the brief.

Wordsworth believed this kind of view could heal all ills, but alas I cannot *feel* its beauty anymore. I went to the doctor who prescribed antidepressants but after a few weeks I threw them away. The pills dulled my senses, and I couldn't write. I would prefer to feel pain than nothing at all.

It's tearing me in two to love and hate at the same time. I long for Alec and I wish never to see him again, but if that wish is granted, I will drown in sorrow.

It has stopped raining and the crows are swooping over the lower ground. On the slopes of the mountain highland cattle graze. I should go out for a walk but tell myself that I must first finish the play. There is only one more scene to write.

The crows have flown away and the cattle lie down in the bracken. Dark clouds roll overhead, ballooning into the sky. A fork of lightning flashes onto the mountain and thunder rumbles round the glen. I watch as the storm reaches its climax; the lightning flickers like a faulty bulb; thunder crashes overhead. It's finished as quickly as it began: the tall clouds sail on to the west. Through the gloom a ray of sunlight struggles through, illuminating the grassy slopes of the hills.

I remove the mawkishness that has wormed its way into the end of the play.

The script is as good as finished but I read through it several times. There is clumsy dialogue to correct. My editor is keen on social realism; likes everything to be short and pithy. I know I have written something mediocre, but I've given him what he wants. I email the play to him—he'll be relieved to receive it: he sends an email back: "Well done. I'll read it tomorrow."

I tidy the study. The weather changes. Low cloud blankets the hills and it is raining. I tell myself it's too late for a walk but really I can't summon up the energy. Later I might use the exercise bike which Alec bought and sat on every day, pedalling relentlessly until he was out of breath and sweating. I thought at the time it was vanity, that he was intent on recapturing his lost youth, but now I think he was chastising himself for a reason I did not then understand.

I have not visited since they took him away. Despite what everyone thinks, I did not suspect his secret. He covered his tracks well, though, as it turned out, not well enough.

It is fortunate that I have fallen out of love with the view because I can no longer afford to live in the house. Tristram and Amanda liked it very much. "I didn't realise you had so many rooms," Amanda said. "In London all we can afford is a tiny flat. Look at you—you have your own study and two spare bedrooms." I didn't tell them that I'm selling up and moving to England.

The rain has lessened to a light drizzle and the crows have returned. Clouds lower over the mountain and hills and the cattle still lie in the bracken. It'll stay light until late in the evening, so I have no excuse for not going outside, but I can't face it.

Today is the first day of the trial.

Sometimes I think he must be innocent, that it's all a mistake, even though the police inspector, sick with disgust, showed me some of the photographs, unbelieving of my protestations of ignorance.

Once sacred, the view is now profane. It's good only for gracing the lid of a biscuit tin. The cattle have roused themselves and graze the lower slopes. Some of the bracken has fully unfurled and a lone oystercatcher, on taut red legs, feeds by the burn. When there were two of us the isolation did not concern me; now I worry about all the things that could go wrong. My nearest neighbour lives nearly three miles away and I have not seen her for weeks.

The estate agent says that eventually someone will love the view, and everything will fall into place. Soon I will have to look for somewhere else to live; near Tristram and Amanda, perhaps, who have stuck by me while most of our friends have fallen away. Tristram said, "If there's anything we can do for you, you only have to ask," and I think he meant it when he said it. Amanda smiled a brittle smile and nodded her agreement.

Alec's solicitor asked me to appear as a defence witness—when I refused, Alec smashed up his cell. He has sent letters I have not opened; I'm too afraid that he will weaken my resolve. After all, he was a professional writer, and a better one than me.

I notice a car on the road, a smart 4x4, too clean to be local. It drives up to the house and a tall man gets out. He's carrying a camera. He walks round the house and I hear him knock on the back door. He waits for a moment, then the gravel crunches under his feet as he returns to the front. I watch him from the office window, carefully, so he can't see me. He knocks, then raises his camera and takes some photos of the house, then he turns and captures the view. Before I know what I'm doing I'm banging my fist on the window. He looks up, and I move back before he can take my photo. He knocks on the door again, then looks at his watch. He gets in the car, turns it round and drives away.

I'm shaking. I've been foolish, thinking the journalists would not bother to come this far north.

A light rain is falling. Swallows dive through the shower, catching the late afternoon midges. The grass bows down with the weight of the rainwater, brushing the sodden, mossy ground.

I open another file and work on the second draft of my novel. At first I can't concentrate, but gradually my hands stop shaking and the words take over so that I don't hear the second car until it drives onto the gravel. A different man knocks on the front door. After a few minutes he walks around to the back of the house and I hear him rooting through the dustbins.

It has stopped raining and the clouds lift from the mountain; it looms once more over the gentler hills. Through my closed window I can hear a blackbird singing and the roar of the burn. The sky is mostly grey, but there are small patches of blue.

The man returns to his car with a carrier bag. What has he found that will be useful to him? Microwave meal trays? Receipts from the shop? Something more incriminating? He puts the bag in the boot and drives away.

The clouds are breaking up and the blackbird still chirps its cheerful song. There is a small movement in the bracken and I catch a glimpse of a deer—a hind—grazing with her faun; just as quickly she disappears.

My novel eludes me so I start work on an article I'm writing for a journal. After a few minutes the phone rings: it's Amanda.

"Are you all right?" she asks.

I tell her about the reporters.

"They're ghouls. Any time you want to come and stay with us, you're more than welcome. We haven't a spare room but you can sleep on the sofa."

"Thank you, Amanda, but I'd prefer to stay here."

"Don't watch the television or listen to the radio. Be nice to yourself. Open a bottle of wine. Light some candles. We'll be thinking of you. By the way, Tristram says, 'How's the view?'"

"It's very much the same as when you were here."

"He says it changed every time he looked at it. That was part of the attraction."

"I've been working today. I've not had time to look out of the window."

Amanda rings off.

There are still three hours of daylight left. A buzzard wheels over the mountain, then soars off to the south. The sky is blue, and sunlight slants over the hills. Tristram would be enchanted, deep in his fairy tale of happiness, lost in the mindful moment of his love. But, despite the view, time will not loosen its grip on me, for I am haunted by the past, and who knows what horrors the future may bring.

Holiday Reading

The book fair was held in the town every August, when many locals were away. Nevertheless, it attracted a good-sized crowd of literature-loving customers augmented by visitors to the town looking for something to do. Most of the latter were perplexed by the antiquarian and collectable modern editions on offer. There was hardly a paperback in sight, Callum noticed as he strolled through the fair, fascinated despite himself. What kind of person bought second hand books on traction engines or keeping geese? Even the fiction was mostly by authors unknown to him. It seemed that book collectors were a whole new, previously unsuspected subset of humanity.

He picked a luridly-covered volume at random from the shelf in front of him. It was *The Haunted Abbey* by Mrs Ashley Galbraith. The blurb was breathless.

Adela Everingham, recovering from a broken engagement, arrives at Aunt Celia's cottage in the country. Exploring the ruins of nearby Sakeby Abbey, Adela meets tall, sardonic soldier Captain Paul Repton, who tells her the story of the ghostly monk that haunts the Abbey. Later, Adela comes across handsome local solicitor Mark Frampton, who intimates that things at the Abbey are not all they seem. In a thrilling climax, Adela must choose between the two explanations of the mystery, and the two men who profess to love her.

Callum looked inside the front of the book for the price. It was £35, far too high for an impulse purchase. He put it back on the shelf and made his way outside. It seemed bright and busy on the street after the hushed gloom of the book fair. He leant against the façade of the town hall, watching the passers-by. It was all very well taking an enforced break, but what the devil was he to do next?

The town was small, with an historic castle, prison and abbey, the first two of which he had visited on the first day of his holiday. He had also gone into some of the charity shops on the high street in search of reading matter, but it seemed that his lassitude made it impossible to find anything that appealed to him, not even amongst the contemporary detective fiction that he usually read. Decisions had become a problem, and his inability to make them the reason why his boss had ordered him to get away from everything for a couple of weeks.

"Everything" included Tessa, who was already showing some signs of impatience with his condition. Doctor Piper had assured him that he had in all probability been working too hard (the Leicester contract had been signed just in time to save the company) and concurred with his boss that he needed a complete change of scene. Tessa had hoped he would take her to Barbados, but he chose instead on a whim to come away on his own to this northern town without even a car to get about in. The hotel was very comfortable, but small, with few facilities. He did not feel like staying in his room watching television, and Doctor Piper had warned him about drinking too much alcohol. That left walking around the town, or taking a train or bus to attractions further afield.

Callum bought himself a cup of coffee at a café. Sitting outside at a table on the pavement he contemplated the rest of his day. There was always the abbey, he supposed, smiling as he remembered *The Haunted Abbey*. Surely every monastic ruin in the country must have its putative ghost.

The abbey was beyond the town to the west, and Callum decided to walk there. It was hot: the midday sun blazed down—he had bought a bottle of water and sipped from it frequently. The abbey ruins lay in an idyllic spot near the river and as Callum drew closer he could see that they were impressive—the church seemed to survive almost to roof height. He bought a guidebook from the kiosk and thoroughly explored the site: there were rare survivals such as the coloured, glazed floor tiles in the church and an almost complete perpendicular window in the refectory. The abbey was constructed of handsome, locally quarried sandstone. There were few other people about, only a family, with two toddlers in a bulky pushchair, and a young woman, who seemed to be on her own. Callum could not help but notice her. Good-looking in a waif-like way, she trailed around listlessly, seemingly only half awake, apparently following in his footsteps, although he noticed that she did not have the guidebook. As he was looking at the floor tiles in the church, she appeared beside him. He glanced at her face and to his dismay saw that she had been crying.

"Is there anything I can do?" he asked diffidently.

"I very much doubt it," she said. "Unless you have a magic wand."

Her voice was low and musical. She took a handkerchief from her blouse pocket and dabbed at her eyes. They were green, Callum noticed, and her hair red. He had never seen such pale, translucent skin.

"I'm afraid I'm not a magician, but I am a good listener," Callum said, putting on his most cheerful voice. "The ruins are rather melancholy, aren't they? But romantic, all the same. Are you on holiday?"

"I've been here many times," she said. "Sometimes I find a sympathetic friend."

"Well I hope that I am that," said Callum.

"I am Gwendoline."

"Callum," said Callum.

Gwendoline had stopped crying.

"Shall we walk together?" she asked.

They strolled somewhat randomly among the ruins. Occasionally, he pointed out a feature. She smiled wanly.

"You seem to know a great deal about the abbey." she said.

"I've read the guidebook."

"There are some things it doesn't include."

Callum laughed. "I suppose there has to be a ghost."

"Yes. Of course. It's of a young woman from the town who was the secret lover of one of the monks. She took to pagan practices and he, in a fit of horror at what she had become, killed her and buried her outside the abbey grounds. She is said to appear only to male visitors."

"I'd better watch out then!"

"Don't worry, I'll protect you."

They had wandered into the monks' dormitory.

"Are you a Christian, Callum?"

"I was a choirboy at school but that was a long time ago."

"But you enjoy visiting old monasteries?"

"They were such impressive buildings in their day, and must have seemed quite alien to the local people."

"The religion of the monks would have been equally foreign."

Gwendoline reached down and picked a piece of tall grass. She shredded the seed head between her fingers.

"Are you feeling better?" he asked.

"A little," she answered, glancing up at him with a flash of a smile.

She sat down on the grass. Callum sank down beside her. She put her arms around his shoulders and nuzzled into his neck. He felt the sharp nip of her teeth. Instinctively he leaned away from her.

"What's the matter?" she asked. "I thought you liked me?"

"I do. It's . . . oh, I don't know!" He put his fingers to the trickle of blood that ran down his neck. "You've broken the skin!"

"I got a bit carried away. I like you, Callum. Why should we wait? You don't have to buy me expensive meals."

Callum was aware that he must seem somewhat priggish. "I have a girlfriend at home."

"She doesn't need to know about me. I don't mind."

Gwendoline put her hand on the back of Callum's head. She looked into his eyes. "Besides, you taste nice."

Callum felt his resistance crumble. He leaned forward and allowed her to kiss him.

❦

Later that afternoon Callum awoke. They had walked to the corner of the field behind the ruins and laid down under the hedge. Gwendoline had gone while he was asleep—there was no trace of her. He put his fingers to his neck. The blood was no longer flowing but he could feel the slight puckering of the wound. Feeling rather foolish now the heat of passion was over, he stood up, brushed himself down and walked back to the abbey. There was no one around: even the kiosk was empty. He began the long trudge to the town.

Callum realised that he had no idea how to find Gwendoline. They had not exchanged phone numbers and she hadn't left a note. Presumably she preferred it that way. He would have liked to see her again—get to know her better. She was an interesting girl and he had enjoyed making love to her, though the truth was that she had made most of the running.

Once he got back to the hotel he was exhausted, and it was all he could do to keep awake for dinner. He ate heartily, however, and felt better. One of the other guests, a woman called April, joined him in the bar afterwards. She, too, was staying at the hotel on her own. Her husband was away on a business trip in the US and she was taking the opportunity to have a short holiday. "It's good not to be in each other's pockets all the time," she said.

Callum found himself telling her about the reasons for his own enforced break. She was very sympathetic. "Burn-out is a terrible thing. Taking a holiday is the best way to deal with it. And this is a good hotel, very discreet." She smiled at him. His eyes were drawn to the red of her lips. He fought against a sudden impulse to lean over and lick them.

He mentioned that he had been to visit the abbey and she laughed. "You know it's meant to be haunted?"

"So I understand."

"It's a story put about to warn people off. After dark, the abbey is a notorious . . . trysting place."

"How do you know all this?"

April laughed. "I have my sources."

Callum found April very easy to talk to. She asked him about himself and he felt no need to hold back. She was a good looking woman, immaculately made up and dressed. It was difficult to guess her age. She mentioned that she did not have any children. It seemed to be the one thing she struggled with.

"We have plenty of room, but it seems that George can't have them. He won't consider adoption, and all the other stuff didn't work." She sighed.

"You haven't considered a donor?" asked Callum. "Wouldn't that be the easiest way?"

"George thinks he might be able to father a child one day, despite what the doctors tell him. He doesn't want to raise someone else's brat."

"You could get pregnant and tell him it was his."

April shook her head. "What a dastardly thing to do, though, Callum."

"Oh, I don't know."

She eyed him speculatively. "You're not offering, are you?"

Callum had drunk several gin and tonics. "Maybe I am." They were alone in the bar. He kissed her neck, then took the tender skin between his teeth.

"Easy," she said.

He took April's hand and allowed her to lead him up to her room.

❧

In the morning Callum found himself back in his own room, although he had no memory of how he had got there. He did remember making love to April, though. At one point she had asked him not to be so rough, though he was sure he had restricted himself to only a few playful nips. The warm taste of her lingered in his mouth. She had thanked him profusely after he had promised never to contact her again. He found it intriguing that even now it was possible that she was carrying his child.

Despite having made love to two women in one day, something that he could not remember having happened before, Callum was filled with an unaccustomed longing. He walked the streets of the town, newly aware of possibilities both obvious and more nebulous.

As he passed the town hall he could see from the posters that the book fair had reached its last day. Inside it was as cool and dim as ever. *The Haunted Abbey* was no longer on its shelf. Instead there were some new pulp titles, *Curse of the Rotten Scoundrel* and *Loud Sings Her Blood*. The stall holder saw him looking at the books.

"You'll not go wrong there," he said.

Callum walked back out into the sunlight, carrying his parcel. A blonde girl was waiting by the door, clutching a bag of books from the fair. He could smell the heady ripeness of her above the mustiness of the old volumes. Just as he caught her eye she smiled at him—he was sure he could hear the blood singing in her veins. He sauntered over.

The break seemed to be doing Callum the world of good.

Sparks from the Fire

The feasting is done and Akui has lit the great fire. See how the flames crackle through the brushwood and sparks fly up into the darkness! Soon the timber will burn and warm us through the night and into the dawn.

Akui says it is my turn to tell the story, but I'm not sure you'll want to listen. I have seen you young people laugh at me when you think my back is turned. To you I am an old dodderer and past anything that matters. Perhaps the elders are right and the old ways are no longer important to you. You care only for your electronic toys and your school books.

There are many ways to tell a story. Many different points of view. It is a question of choosing the right one. I am not a natural wordsmith. On my evenings with the elders I listen, but I do not speak. Maybe I should stare into the fire for a while and think the story through, untangle the knots and smooth it out in my mind to my own satisfaction. But then there would be silence and no guarantee of a story at the end of it.

So we will see how it unravels. The hunt was successful and your bellies are full and it is too much effort for you to move away from the fire, so maybe you will listen for a while, and doze. And I will ramble on, as old men do, and fulfil the obligation Akui has entrusted to me.

Not all people have lived as we do now. In days gone by the rules were different, often stricter, and the taboos more carefully policed.

Tura, a maiden of seventeen years, had grown weary of the surveillance she and the other girls suffered from the older women. She could not even speak to a young man without a chaperone taking her arm and leading her sharply away. Tura was the daughter of an elder, and so was expected to behave extra cautiously and well, as befitted her status and as an example to the girls of lesser caste.

Tura's father had died, and despite her status she was put to work—milling the grain and mixing the flour with water and frying the bread. She was taught to spin and weave the fine cloth that the women wore. Life was harder then and everyone, even the children, had to do their bit, fetching water from the creek. The menfolk herded the goats and once each quarter went hunting with spears for gazelles. And if the hunt was successful the whole village feasted and celebrated under the full moon, as if they were as free as they had been before the mundane settled life and the growing of grain and the herding of goats.

Tura's father had been a great hunter, although he was not always an easy man to know. He often shirked his responsibilities and went walkabout in the bush. He was tolerated by the others because of his skill in the hunt, and because he reminded them of the old days, in the far distant past, when hunting had been the way of life of the tribe.

Tura longed to go hunting. She was tall and strong and could run without becoming tired. She was sure she would not be a burden to the men, but she knew that they would never take her. This was the strictest taboo of all, for the boys were initiated on the hunting trips, and received the markings on their cheeks that made them men.

So Tura wove and spun and milled the grain to make the bread, and watched the young men as they herded the goats and prepared themselves for the hunt. And she grew angry and bitter at her lot. For it had been decided that it was time for her to take a husband, and in those days she had no say in who that would be. As she assessed the young men who enjoyed a status equal to her own, none of them seemed worthy of her, and in her pride she grew surly and rarely smiled. At last her mother spoke to her.

"Why, Tura, are you so glum, when your wedding day approaches? You should be looking forward to all that it will bring."

Tura sobbed, "Oh Mother, I don't want to be married!"

"Nonsense, girl," her mother tut-tutted. "You will be married and learn to like it. It has already been decided who your spouse will be."

"Don't tell me, Mother, I don't want to know!"

Tura's mother sighed and stroked her daughter's hair. "This marriage will come to pass, so reconcile yourself to it."

The year moved on and it was time for another hunt: the men were painting the swirling designs on their bodies in readiness, allowing the women and dogs to guard the goats. It was harvest time and out in the fields the women scythed the wheat and pushed it into rows to dry. Everywhere women were working and the men were sharpening their spears and talking themselves into a state of readiness. As she went about her work Tura watched the men carefully. Only one caught her eye, a tall young man called Selim, who had no caste and was quieter than the rest. As a child, Selim had run away from another village and been taken in by the elders. He was forced to work harder than any man. Despite his lowly origins he had forged a reputation for honesty and skill at hunting. It had been regarded as a great honour for him when he was initiated into the tribe. Tura knew that his lowly status meant that he would not be the man already picked as her husband.

Then Tura thought she could hear her father's voice. "Be brave, Tura, and chase your dreams. For you are truly the daughter of Idris, who hunts now in the starry heavens."

That night, as the hunter's moon rose in the darkening sky, Tura slipped away from her hut. The men had gathered at the far end of the village, ready to venture out into the bush. From somewhere in the middle distance a lion roared—a sure sign that gazelle were close by—the men would not be the only hunters out that night. Tura followed the men as they silently padded out through the scrub. It took all her concentration not to lose them, and to walk quietly, even when she trod on a thorn and had to stop and draw it out. After some time the hunters stood still—they were listening intently—then they began to gesticulate to each other in an elaborate mime. In the light of the moon they spread out into a wide arc and held their spears at the ready. Tura found that she was holding her breath. As she looked across the plain she was horrified to see a lioness crouched and ready to spring at one of the oblivious hunters. With no time to think she shouted "Look out!"—the hunter—it was Selim, turned and threw his spear: it missed and the lioness slunk off, unhurt.

Selim ran over to Tura. "Whatever are you doing here?" he asked. His eyes gleamed in the moonlight.

"I wanted to go on a hunt . . . " said Tura lamely.

"You saved my life," he said, "but you have broken the taboo. Perhaps if you go home now, all will be well."

Tura hung her head forlornly. Selim took hold of her hand and squeezed it. "Off you go."

Tura retraced her steps back to the village. Dawn was close, and she barely had time to slip back into the hut and lay down among her sleeping sisters before the sun came up. Soon she was at the quern, grinding the grain. The hunters had returned empty handed, so there was no celebration, no feasting, no fire. By the afternoon the men had washed the coloured earth from their bodies and were again taking the goats out to pasture. Tura watched the women winnowing the grain.

Tura's mother came to meet her at the end of the day. "We have chosen your future husband and it is time for you to be introduced. Be ready after our meal tonight."

"But, mother . . . "

Her mother's patience snapped. "Don't 'but mother' me! You will be ready and you will look your best or you'll have me to answer to."

So Tura put on her bangles and her finest cloth and painted white spirals on her cheeks. After her meal she went to her mother's hut and sat and waited for her future husband to arrive. Time passed and still he did not come. Tura's mother began to fidget, and looked out toward the setting sun.

"Where can he be?" she asked.

Etiquette meant that she could not go and look for the man, for he must come freely or not at all. After the sun had set, she lit the little tallow lamp and they waited again. Tura dared to hope that he would not come. Her mother was already furious at the slight of unpunctuality. What would she be like if he did not come at all!

It dawned on Tura that her future husband could have heard about her following the hunters. She had spoken to Selim without a chaperone being present. Her reputation must be in tatters amongst the men. Some of them would have seen or heard her in the bush.

Tura's mother was distraught. It had taken many days to negotiate the marriage. Now all that effort was wasted, and the family had lost face. The village gossips had much to work on, and soon Tura's reputation was ruined. She had brought shame on her family, and broken one of the strongest of all the taboos.

At first Tura did not care about her reputation, and she was pleased that she would not be getting married. But then she began to notice the few unmarried women in the village—those shamed in some way or too ill or ugly—and how they were spurned by all. Even those of high caste. These women were forced to do the most uncongenial work. This gave Tura pause for thought. She had believed that her youth and good looks would protect her, but it occurred to her now that she would not be young for ever.

And so Tura entered a new stage in her life, where she was fearful and chastened, but fought to improve her reputation by hard work and wise living. On hunting nights she still felt the pull of desire, but told herself that it was all in the past. She worked hard and was respectful to her elders and by and large she was content.

But still she prayed to her father for some way out of her present life.

One night, when she had slipped away and was walking back to her hut via the corral, she almost bumped into Selim, whose turn it was to guard the goats. She looked down at the ground, as the taboo dictated. He laughed and said, "I have been watching you. You work hard and you are very respectful, but no one will marry you except me."

Tura looked up in surprise. She realised then that it must have been Selim who told everyone about her following the hunt. He was smiling down at her and she thought, *He loves me.* Slowly and carefully she looked him in the eyes and smiled right back at him, the smile of an equal. Over the next few days Tura could feel Selim's eyes on her. Soon afterwards he asked for Tura's hand, and Tura's family were so pleased to be rid of her that they agreed at once.

So Tura and Selim were married, and before Selim went hunting, he always said thanks for the time he was saved from a lioness by Tura. Even her many children did not stop Tura from wanting to go on the hunt. There were some misgivings in the village that Tura had married below her caste, and this was seen to account for the fact that

Selim and Tura had an unusual marriage. The two of them discussed every decision and came to an agreement about how to proceed, rather than Selim laying down the law like the other men. And because they generally made good decisions, their way of going about things spread to some of the other families in the village. And this is how the old taboos shifted their shapes, and how you young girls and boys have won your freedom to go to school, take jobs in the city, and choose who to marry.

And please do not in your new-fangled lives forget the hunting and feasting, and the lighting of the fire, and remember if you can an old man telling a story, his words as fleeting as the sparks that fly.

The Birdcage

The Birdcage was one of the surprisingly large number of establishments listed in directories of the most haunted pubs of England. It acquired its name during the Napoleonic Wars, when it was a jail for captured French soldiers. Since then it had returned to its former use as a tavern, the medieval timber-framing and beams ensuring that it was popular with those who liked to drink in a pub with plenty of character. Some customers, however, came because of the poltergeist, which was reputed to cause glasses to fly through the air and smash against the walls.

Carol and Sean took over the tenancy of The Birdcage a few weeks before Christmas. The pub was well set up, with reliable staff and a good chef. It just needed titivating here and there—new chairs and a rearrangement of the dining room. The previous tenants, Sue and Jeff, were retiring from the trade, and arranged for Carol and Sean an extended and comprehensive handover. They stressed the importance of the tourist trade, and the inclusion of the pub as a stopping point on several ghost tour coach trips. Smaller parties of tourists tended to eat in the pub and sometimes stayed the night in the four bedrooms. It was mainly the food that made the business profitable. Sue suggested that they could theme the meals and rooms around the poltergeist, but perhaps that was going too far.

The first coach party of Chinese tourists arrived on a Monday lunchtime. The tour guide and translator, Lin, was a smartly-dressed English-woman of Chinese descent. There was a certain difficulty in fitting thirty people in the smallish public bar, but they didn't seem to mind that it was standing room only. Lin explained about the poltergeist and photographs were taken of the bar. The tourists then began to order, with Lin's help, halves of bitter and sandwiches. There was a contented cacophony of Cantonese. As Carol took the orders through to chef, she felt the only thing that was missing from a very profitable lunchtime service was the poltergeist itself. Neither she nor Sean had heard the ghost, and she was unsure if that was a good thing. If they were to rest much of their reputation on the poltergeist, then she felt it would be useful if it occasionally manifested itself. On the other hand, it might be quite upsetting and frightening if it did. Sue and Jeff had been reticent about the ghost, claiming it had only once been active during their tenure, when one evening two full pints of bitter had been mysteriously knocked off the counter.

Carol and Sean posed for several photos and then the Chinese group departed, leaving the public bar to be cleared and cleaned.

That evening was quiet, with only a few regulars drinking at the bar. Jeremy Taylor sipped his pint of bitter.

"I heard you had a coach load at lunch time," he said to Sean. "Good business for you."

"Yes," agreed Sean.

"They came to see the poltergeist I expect," said Jeremy. "I don't suppose it obliged?"

"It didn't," said Sean.

"You know, we could rig something up, knock over a few pints for you, no trouble."

"Thank you, Jeremy, but I think we'll give it a miss. You can imagine the bother we'd be in if it got out that we were faking it."

"I was in here one night when it did kick off," said Sol Blandford. "It made a hell of a mess, chucking pints against the wall there. I reckon it must be an angry soul. One of those prisoners of war, I expect, that was locked up here."

Later, when closing time had passed and they were alone behind the bar, Carol said, "It wouldn't be a bad idea, faking the ghost I mean. We could film it on my phone and post it on YouTube. It would be great for trade. Think about it, Sean."

Sean scratched his chin. "I'm not sure. Word would be bound to get out that we'd rigged it and it would cause more trouble than it's worth."

"Come on, Sean, no publicity is bad publicity. If we're going to make this place work we need more tourists."

The idea was left unresolved between them.

Trade before Christmas was brisk, but they could see from the books that the pub was only just profitable. They had a visit from one more Chinese coach party and it was as successful as the first. Another would have been more than useful. Despite holding a weekly music evening, when customers could bring their own instruments to play, and a quiz night, they were not attracting enough people who wanted to eat. It was an unavoidable fact that their unique selling point was the poltergeist and they were failing to promote it adequately.

So Carol and Sean found themselves with Jeremy Taylor filming as, with the aid of a simple contraption of string and Sellotape, two pints of bitter were seemingly knocked off the bar by an invisible force. Carol posted the footage on their Facebook page, and on YouTube with the comment, "Spooky goings on at The Birdcage. Invisible pint spiller disrupts drinkers at our medieval pub." As Carol predicted, it soon had thousands of views, and the local radio station came to interview them. In the two weeks before Christmas trade improved by fifty per cent, with many more tourists eating in the pub. Even after Christmas, customer numbers held up, although there was no more poltergeist activity, real or rigged, to help things along.

Carol went ahead with theming the rooms and food and they continued to take more bookings. Profits were up and all seemed to be going well.

The first sign of trouble came in the Friday edition of the local paper, where a short paragraph caught Sean's attention.

"All is not quite as it seems at The Birdcage public house, where sources suggest that recent YouTube footage of their resident poltergeist was faked by a local drinker and the landlord and lady, Sean and Carol Dennis. A shabby trick indeed."

Sean called his wife over. "I knew it would end in tears."

Carol swallowed. "Jeremy must've talked. They'll have got him drunk."

"What do we do now?"

"We pretend it was all tongue in cheek. No one was supposed to take it seriously."

So they fronted it out, and the strategy seemed to work. The local paper printed a largely sympathetic interview in which they admitted the ruse, and views of the footage continued to rise. Now the tourists came to see where the video had been made. Bookings increased and they had to hire another assistant for the kitchen. In the evenings the pub was heaving with local drinkers and tourists. Jeremy Taylor apologised for spilling the beans about the video: unsurprisingly he had been drinking with the journalist, who it turned out had already smelt a rat.

When Carol came downstairs one morning she at first could not work out what had happened. Broken glass lay all over the floor of the pubic bar and bottles were strewn over the counter and shelves. She thought there must have been a break in, but when she tried the doors, they were still locked. As she and Sean cleared up, she said, "You know what this is, don't you? It's the poltergeist."

"Don't be soft," said Sean, "someone must've got in through a window."

"They're all locked too."

Sean blinked.

Carol said, "It must've been angry that we faked it."

"You do talk rubbish," said Sean uncertainly. "You don't really believe in the damn thing, do you?"

Carol looked at him in surprise. "Of course I do. Sue and Jeff saw it, didn't they?"

"I thought they might've made that up to impress us."

"Several of the regulars have been in when it kicked off."

"So they say."

"Well how do you explain all this mess if it isn't the poltergeist?"

Sean had no answer. Once they had cleared it up, Carol suggested that they should set up CCTV cameras in the bar. Much to her surprise, Sean agreed and spent the rest of the day researching on the internet and purchasing a system. It arrived by courier the following day, and Sean spent several hours after lunch installing it.

"We'll soon get to the bottom of your poltergeist," he said to Carol.

However, nothing further happened, except that bookings held up and Carol and the chef changed the menu so that it included more high-end, extra-profitable dishes. After Easter, the coach tours started up again, and more of them arranged to stop off at The Birdcage, which was conveniently situated between London and Stratford-Up-on-Avon. In April a party of German tourists called in; they mainly drank quantities of bottled lager and ordered fish and chips. When it was explained that there weren't enough fish to go round there was a mini riot in the bar, although it was largely good natured once they were steered onto other dishes. Gunther spoke the best English.

"We wanted to see, or should I say hear, your famous poltergeist. Do you think it could be arranged?"

Carol laughed. "Oh, it can't be summoned up, it has a will of its own. It hasn't been active for several months. But you never know . . . you might be lucky if you stay long enough."

Gunther grinned. "Then I'll have another of these lagers, please."

The party stayed for another three hours, despite the best efforts of the tour guide to get them back on the coach.

Five days later the German tourists stopped again, on their way back from touring the west of England. Gunther greeted Carol like an old friend.

"We have stopped at many haunted pubs but none were as atmospheric as The Birdcage."

They ordered fish and chips and pies, and more bottles of lager. It seemed they hadn't experienced hauntings at any of the pubs they stopped at. Gunther was sanguine about this, saying, "We are so noisy it would frighten the devil away."

And indeed it would have been possible to miss the poltergeist when it finally put in an appearance towards the end of the lunchtime service. The tourist party were well lubricated by then and singing German songs. Carol felt a sudden drop in temperature behind the bar—she reached for her cardigan—and then all hell let loose, with glasses falling off the counter and smashing against the walls. Several of the German tourists didn't realise what was happening and, thinking it was some local custom, threw their lager bottles onto the floor. Gunther came running in from the dining room.

"It's the ghost, isn't it, Carol?" he said, surveying the scene of devastation.

Sean came into the bar from the dining room just as the manifestation ceased.

"What's happened here?" he asked.

"It's the poltergeist," said Gunther. "Perhaps it doesn't like our singing."

Sean turned to Carol. "It's real," she said. "I saw it."

Sean was baffled. "Are you having me on?" he asked.

"No, I swear. Those glasses smashed against the wall by themselves. Can't you feel how cold it is?"

Sean shuddered briefly and swore. He took out his mobile and found the number of their local journalist.

As there were several other eyewitnesses prepared to talk to the reporter, a lengthy article appeared in the local newspaper, which was picked up by the nationals. Soon the story was all over social media and ghost-themed blogs. The Birdcage had its moment of fame, or notoriety, depending on your point of view. It was very good for business.

From that day onward, Carol and Sean came downstairs every morning to a mess of broken glass and disarranged bottles in the public bar. Carol soon grew sick of all the work entailed in cleaning it up. The CCTV had stopped working and despite spending an afternoon dismantling the cameras and checking the wiring, Sean could not mend it. He sent the whole system back to the internet trader he had bought it from.

"I'd like to know what this is all about," said Sean. "If it is one of those prisoners of war then were they badly treated, I wonder? Do you think we can do something to appease him so that he stops smashing up the bar?"

In the end they called in the vicar of St. Mary's who was persuaded, rather against her will, to perform a blessing. Carol filmed the ceremony surreptitiously on her phone, and posted it on Facebook. Things quietened down for a few days and just as they were beginning to believe that the blessing had been effective, the mayhem started up again. This time glasses were flung at the wall while a coach party of British ghost hunters were in the pub. A shard of broken glass nicked the hand of a woman from Birmingham and the small but deep wound began to bleed profusely. Carol bandaged it up as best she could, and offered the woman and her husband a meal on the house. The woman was quite upset, despite being a ghost enthusiast. It seemed she assumed they had set up the glass smashing as a stunt.

"If customers are going to be injured then it is no laughing matter," Carol said to Sean that evening.

"But what can we do?" he replied. "The blessing hasn't worked—do we start looking for an exorcist?"

"Maybe it's something simple he needs, like food. They can't have fed prisoners of war very well in those days."

"So what are we going to do?" asked Sean. "Leave a steak and ale pie on the bar?"

"Why not?" said Carol. "Unless you can think of anything better."

So that evening Carol heated up one of chef's pies and left it, gently steaming, on the counter. In the morning the pie was still there, untouched and congealed, the public bar around it in perfect order. That was the beginning of the ritual which Carol and Sean carried out every night—leaving a hot pie on the counter for the poltergeist. The food was never touched, but they had no more trouble from the unruly spirit. It was a small price to pay. Soon, coach parties of ghost enthusiasts stayed until closing time to watch the ceremony of the appeasing pie.

Business continued to boom.

Tour Guide

The sand shimmered and sparkled under the midday sun. Millicent wriggled her toes in her sandals and looked up at Fabian as he addressed the party of tourists. Behind them, the calm blue sea rippled rhythmically over the beach.

"If you would like to, we can walk across the bay to the sub-tropical gardens on the other side of the island. Or we can stop here and eat our packed lunches. It's up to you. Discuss it amongst yourselves and come back to me."

There was an embarrassed silence, and then a low thrum of disjointed consultation.

"I think I'm right in saying," said Jim Clair eventually, "that most of us would like to walk to the sub-tropical gardens."

There was a rumble of agreement.

"Very well," said Fabian, "then please follow me."

Millicent raised her hand. "Could I just ask . . . ?"

"Fire away!"

" . . . is there ever any frost on the islands?"

"That's a good question, Millicent. There have been occasional below zero days and nights which have resulted in a lot of frost damage to the sub-tropical plants. But for the last fifteen years we have been frost free and the plants are thriving."

Elsa Clair took hold of Millicent's arm. She whispered, "Leave Fabian alone for five minutes can't you? It's becoming embarrassing."

Millicent pulled her arm away. "Nonsense, Mummy, tour guides like to answer questions. It's part of their job." She skipped up to the front of the already straggling procession of tourists. Fabian smiled at her distractedly. He was trying to recall the names of some of the plants in the sub-tropical gardens. Someone—Millicent most likely—was bound to ask and botany was not his specialism. He took out his mobile phone and began searching online.

"Remember to drink plenty of water," he called out. "It's a very hot day."

Millicent took a dutiful swig from her bottle. "How many plants are in the gardens, Fabian?"

Fabian tapped into his phone. "According to the website there are 20,000 different plants. It's called the Abbey Garden because it was planted on the site of an old monastery."

"Do you like being a tour guide?" Millicent asked, studying Fabian's long dark eyelashes.

"I like meeting people who are interested in learning about the Scilly Isles and Tresco. I grew up here. I had to go to school on the mainland by boat every day. Imagine that!"

"It sounds much nicer than my horrid boarding school. I have to stay away from home for weeks on end. Mummy and daddy won't let me go to the local school, even though it's perfectly all right."

"I expect they think boarding school is character forming."

"My character's already formed. They say you are shaped by the time you're seven, and I'm twelve."

They walked around some low sand dunes. The sun beat down on the top of their heads.

"When are we going to have our sandwiches?"

"We'll wait until we reach the gardens. There's some shade there. It's no more than a mile or so."

Millicent raced to the top of a dune and looked back at the drift of tourists behind them. "Mr. and Mrs. Brownlee are a long way behind. Do you think they're all right?"

"They'll be fine if we let them walk at their own pace."

"I'm not going to get old," said Millicent, "I've decided." She ran down the dune and landed at Fabian's side. "How old are you, Fabian?"

"Never you mind!"

"Did you go to university?"

"I'm at university. This is my summer vacation job."

"What are you studying?"

"Geography."

"Oh. It could be worse, I suppose."

Elsa Clair caught up with her daughter. "I do hope, Fabian, that Millicent isn't too annoying?"

"She's fine. It makes the job more interesting having someone keen tagging along."

The party of tourists now stretched out behind Fabian in a long caravan across the sand.

"I suppose we had better wait here for some of the stragglers to catch up," he said.

Elsa took off her jacket and folded it over her arm. She shook out her hair, then sat down on the dune.

"I must say, Fabian, I'm ravenously hungry."

"We'll eat as soon as we reach the gardens."

"I hope these gardens are all they're cracked up to be. I've been to Kew and I don't see how they could compare."

"Oh mummy, they're lovely. I saw some photographs on Fabian's phone."

Jim Clair caught up with them and sat down next to his wife.

"It really is very hot. Do you know the exact temperature?"

Fabian sighed. "I imagine it's around the mid-twenties. Maybe more."

"A bit warm for some of these oldies, don't you think?"

"Most people are properly dressed for the weather, and have hats," said Fabian pointedly.

Jim smoothed his thinning hair. "What is the tour company's policy on days like this? Surely we shouldn't be undertaking much in the way of physical activity?"

"The company leaves it up to individual tour guides to decide what's for the best. It really is less than a mile now. And you voted to walk to the gardens."

Jim cleared his throat. "It wasn't a vote, exactly . . . "

The tour party gathered around Fabian.

"I suggest that we rest for five minutes, then continue on," he said.

"It is terribly hot," said Mrs. Brownlee. Mr. Brownlee was wearing a knotted handkerchief on his head. Water bottles were passed round.

Sanjay Bangalore smiled at Fabian. "Tresco is quite a small island, isn't it?"

"Yes, it's a mile and a half long."

Sanjay turned to his wife: "You see, we couldn't get lost, even if we wanted to."

"Of course we won't get lost," said Fabian. "All we have to do is walk round the bay and we'll be there. I've done it dozens of times. None of you are to worry."

"And the boat will come to take us back to St. Mary's?"

"It will. Now, time's up. Let's get walking."

Fabian walked very slowly to make sure the Brownlees didn't fall behind again. After twenty-five minutes they reached the Abbey Gardens. Sitting in the shade of a clump of palm trees they took out their packed lunches, provided by the hotel. They each had cheese and pickle sandwiches, a packet of crisps, a chocolate bar, and an apple. The chocolate bars had melted in the heat.

"It's not very nice, is it," said Millicent, who nevertheless ate everything.

The gardens seemed to be deserted. Fabian handed round simple maps.

"The plants are arranged on two terraces, an upper and a lower, screened from the salt spray of the sea by a shelter belt, which you can see here. The boat will be collecting us from the beach to the north in an hours' time, so I'd like to suggest that we meet back here at 2:15, which should give us plenty of time to look round."

Fabian walked down the steps to the lower terrace. The tour party followed him.

"Do you like the gardens, Fabian?" asked Elsa.

"They're very impressive," he replied.

"Does that mean he likes them?" asked Mr. Brownlee.

"I'm not sure," answered Sanjay.

"You'd think he'd know by now," grumbled Mrs. Brownlee.

Fabian had hoped that everyone would be happy to wander around without him. Elsa took his arm. "It's rather marvellous, with these succulent plants in flower. It feels almost natural for them to be running riot like this."

"They've all been planted over the last one hundred and fifty years. Very few of them would grow here without careful management and the shelter belt."

Millicent pointed at a gaudy scarlet bloom. "What's that one called?"

"I don't know," said Fabian. "If we spot one of the gardeners they'll be able to tell us."

The rest of the party clustered round with their questions.

"What is the largest plant in the garden?"

"It feels like a jungle, doesn't it? Are we the only people here?"

"Do they have to water the plants?"

"Are there any carnivorous plants?"

Which plant has been here the longest?"

Fabian noticed Mr. Fordyce surreptitiously taking cuttings from some of the plants and putting them into a plastic bag.

"Please don't touch the plants or take samples," he called out, "or we may be asked to leave."

"I'm not doing any harm," said Mr. Fordyce. "It's not as if I'm digging them up."

"Where are the gardeners?" asked Sanjay. "I would like to ask some questions, and so would my wife."

"I expect they're on their lunch break."

They had reached the cooler lower terrace, where the plants were from more temperate climes. Fabian extracted himself from Elsa's grip.

"Why don't you have a look round on your own? You have your maps to guide you, and it's almost impossible to get lost."

There was a brief silence. Jim Clair cleared his throat. "We have chosen to come on a tour with a tour guide, Fabian. All we're asking is for you to do your job."

"As I've already explained," said Fabian, "I am not an expert on the garden. I can't answer most of your questions. You'd be better off walking round on your own. If you'd like to write down your questions I'll try to find one of the gardeners to answer them for you before we leave."

Fabian used the slight hiatus caused by his announcement to stride away from the group. He aimed towards a low masonry arch which formed the entrance to a vaulted medieval cellar, part of the ruins of the monastery that pre-dated the gardens by almost three-hundred years. Glancing around to make sure he had not been followed, he took the steps down to the cool, dark room. He leaned his back against the wall, took out a pack of cigarettes and lit one. He could hear loud shouts and cries percolating down from the garden. The cries seemed to be increasingly animal and raucous. He smoked his cigarette. Several minutes later he sensed that someone had joined him in the cellar—he could hear quick breaths being taken.

"Millicent, is that you?"

"You don't want to know what's going on up there. My parents have completely lost the plot. You'll have to go up, Fabian."

"I'm staying down here until it blows itself out. There's no stopping them when they're in this sort of mood."

"What do you mean?

"It's a kind of herd mentality. It's best to keep out of their way. They have to blunder around on their own and tire themselves out. Then they'll get in the boat and we can take them back to the hotel. They won't remember much about it afterwards."

"Mummy was . . . doing something with Mr. Bangalore! And daddy . . . "

"It can all get a bit out of hand."

Millicent was silent for a while. The bellowing and shouting continued from above. Fabian dropped his cigarette onto a pile of stubs and ground it out under his boot.

"Does it happen every time?"

"No."

"I don't want to grow up, Fabian."

Gradually the noises died away. Fabian took Millicent's hand and led her to the steps.

"I think it's safe now. Come on."

As they emerged into the garden, the tour party were standing together not far from the entrance to the cellar. They seemed rather subdued.

"It's time to go and find our boat, but before we do, has any one written down any questions?"

There was only silence. Some people hung their heads.

"Good," said Fabian. "Then let's go."

The tour party turned as one and slowly headed to the beach.

Wing Man

Like most children I dreamed I could fly—and that I could take giant bounding leaps across the landscape. On summer mornings I would try this out on my way to school, hoping to find myself far above the tarmacked lane, looking down on the fields and my friends below. At best I achieved a sort of yogic skip, which gave me a certain thrill, though obviously not the full flying experience of my dreams.

Each summer I dream again of flying and my giant strides. The dreams are presaged early in May by the arrival of the swifts, those fantastically manoeuvrable little birds that do almost everything on the wing. I watch them in the evenings from the conservatory, where my wheelchair sits for most of the summer. It stays comfortably warm in here, even when Sheila opens all the windows.

I am not completely inactive—I am a member of a wheelchair rugby team and have competed in the London Marathon. It is three years since the incident that confined me to a wheelchair. It is true that you can get used to most things, and in many ways I live a full life, with Sheila's help. But there are some things that are impossible to fully accept.

Sheila is a good looking woman, and I know that I am lucky that she has stuck by me. But things haven't always been so clear cut. Three years ago, before the accident, I was a sales executive, selling mobile phones to the Middle East, flying out to the Arab states every few weeks. When

I was home I played on the wing for Wonley Rugby Union Football Club, my local amateur side, and that is what I lived and breathed for. I had played rugby for my school and university, in the same position. I was slippery and quick and lucky enough to be one of the best players at the Club, winning player of the year three years running.

I met Sheila at a rugby club dance—she was there with Matt Ridgely, our scrum half. Matt wasn't too keen on me after that, and it caused some bad feeling in the team. It was summer, so we were not playing competitive matches but training, the squad meeting up two evenings each week at the Club. I tried talking to Matt, but he said, "You stole her from me, Ben: that's all there is to it."

We were playing sevens and Matt was on the opposite team. I knew as soon as he thundered into me that some of my ribs were broken. They strapped me up at the hospital and the doctor told me not to train for at least three months. I was feeling pretty sore, and spent a few days at home. Sheila and I fell out over some petty things—I did not take my enforced idleness well. A couple of weeks later I heard from a mutual friend that Sheila had been seen out with Matt.

I went back to work and after a few days preparation in the office flew out to Abu Dhabi. Two hours into the flight there was an unexpected thunderstorm and so much turbulence that the plane was flung violently around. At one point we went into a nose dive, and the oxygen masks snaked down from the panel above. I prided myself on being a good flier, but I admit that I was scared. I thought we were going to die.

Almost as soon as it had started it was over. We somehow got through the rest of the flight and landed safely. I had a good few days showcasing our latest mobile phone and taking orders from the retail suppliers, then flew back to Heathrow. I was given a window seat overlooking the wing.

It started even before take-off—the sweating and swallowing and shaking. Once we were airborne, I was in a full-blown panic attack, my eyes shut, gulping down air in jagged breaths. A flight attendant noticed my distress and talked me through the worst of it, although it didn't get much better for the rest of the flight. I couldn't say it was a fear of any one thing in particular, just a visceral response to flying. I was fine as soon as my feet touched the ground.

From then on I suffered the same problem every time I flew. I learnt to manage it better, but the same terror lay just beneath the surface. After a while I began to find excuses for not flying. Eventually I told Sheila about it (we had mostly made up by then), and she suggested I should see a hypnotherapist.

We found Saul McCabe on the internet. His website claimed that he could help with almost any phobia. He had a consulting room in a building just off Wandsworth High Street. I didn't know what to expect, but he turned out to be a very ordinary looking middle-aged man with a quiet voice. He shook my hand, and asked me to sit down in a comfortable armchair.

"I may not be able to cure you," he said, "but your problem is more common than you might think and I've a good record in ameliorating the worst of the symptoms."

He asked me to talk about my earliest experiences of flying. I told him about my childhood dreams of the giant strides, of early holidays with my parents, about my job. He asked me to close my eyes and carry on talking. I felt calm and increasingly dreamy and occasionally I was aware that McCabe was speaking. After half an hour he put a hand on my shoulder and asked for his fee.

I told Sheila that I didn't know how the therapy had gone. I certainly felt no different. I went to one more session with McCabe before I was next due to fly. It was as low key as the first. I sat in the armchair and he asked me again to tell him about all my experiences of flying. I found myself talking about the thunderstorm. At the end he wished me good luck and took my cash as before.

The flight to Abu Dhabi was delayed by nearly three hours and I sat in the terminal in some trepidation. Finally the flight was called and we boarded the plane. I could feel some of the old fear, but it was muffled, at a distance. I was able to concentrate on reading sales reports. Occasionally I found the courage to look out of the window. It seemed that my money hadn't been wasted.

On my return, back in my own bed, the dreams began. I was seven years old, practicing my giant strides in the lane on the way to school, only this time my leaps grew effortlessly longer and higher until I was bounding into the air, the road a thin ribbon of grey far beneath me. I was a swan flying in a V formation, navigating along the shining sinuous course of the river below. I was a WWII bomber pilot, following the same river in the moonlight to a distant target. Night after night the dreams continued and elaborated. I grew restless, impatient for my next flight.

Sheila said, "I think you should go back to Saul, he needs to put you in reverse." But I liked the fact that my fear had gone and didn't want to do anything to jeopardise it.

I relished flying for work again, and found any excuse to do so. My ribs healed and I was back in training at the Club. The season was due to start in a couple of weeks. Matt seemed to have become more accepting of me and Sheila. She told me that she had only agreed to have a few drinks with him because she felt sorry for him.

Against Sheila's wishes I had joined a gliding club with the aim of qualifying for a glider pilot's licence. Soon I was taking the controls in a two-man glider, learning from Bill, my instructor, how to ride the thermals, and to bring the craft down safely on the bumpy airfield. It was a fabulous experience to be up in the sky without an engine, reliant on your own reactions and skill. Sheila did not like to think of me up there with so little control—I took her concern as a compliment. She still seemed to think I needed looking after.

On the Monday before our first Rugby match I flew out to Dubai International from Gatwick. Again I was allocated the window seat that overlooked the wing. Any kind of flying was a pure pleasure for me then. I inserted my earphones, closed my eyes and listened to some music while the plane taxied and took off. As we were levelling out I distinctly heard a familiar quiet voice say:

"Open your eyes and look out of the window."

The voice repeated:

"Look out of the window."

I opened my eyes. Saul McCabe, dressed in his usual jacket and jeans, was sitting cross-legged on the wing, his hair buffeted by the wind. He turned his head to look at me.

"Is it natural for us to fly," the voice asked, "when we have wings?"

At that moment McCabe unfurled two huge, white feathered wings from his back. He shook them out, paused for a second and then launched himself into the air, swooping and diving into the wind, circling the aircraft and looping underneath and round. He landed on the aeroplane's wing and sat down, folding his wings back into place.

"You should try it, Ben," the voice said. "There's nothing like freeform flying. It beats your giant strides."

The next thing I knew I was out on the wing with him, unfurling my own wings then jumping off after him into the blue. It was more than exhilarating, it was terrifying and stupendous and electrifying and I adored every second of it. I followed McCabe's lead, and he took me through the manoeuvres I had seen him perform solo. Too soon we landed back on the aeroplane's wing. McCabe turned to me and said, "You have earned your wings." We sat companionably for a few minutes, the wind blasting into us. Then McCabe reached over and put his hand on my shoulder and said, "It's time for me to go now."

And I was back in my seat, reaching for the paper bag into which I was horribly sick. The flight attendant brought me a glass of water. When I steeled myself to look out of the window again there was no sign of McCabe. My iPod was playing music again and none of the other passengers showed any signs of having seen anything unusual.

For the rest of the flight I sat in fear that I was having a seizure or episode of some kind. What I had experienced felt so real. I gradually calmed down and by the time we landed I convinced myself that I had been prey to some kind of induced waking dream. I resolved to have it out with McCabe on my return to England.

My business trip was successful—Dubai was one of our best markets—and the flight back to Gatwick was uneventful. Sheila surprised me by meeting me at the airport. I was a little wary of her because I suspected that she was involved with whatever had happened on the outward flight. I was also unclear as to whether or not she was still seeing Matt.

The rugby season began and we beat Rocastle 21 to 17. Sheila celebrated on the side lines as, just before half time, I scored a try. Matt Ridgely had withdrawn from the team not long before the start of the game. Afterwards we enjoyed a few drinks in the Club bar. I'd drunk several pints and finally found the courage to ask Sheila what she and McCabe had done to my iPod. She looked puzzled, then said:

"I don't know what you're talking about, Ben, but I've been meaning to tell you: Saul disappeared just over a week ago. I tried phoning him a few times and then I read about it in the newspaper—he's done a bunk and no one knows where he's gone."

Sheila drove me home soon afterwards.

The next day the Club secretary phoned and told me that Matt had resigned and joined our local rivals, Grantly RUFC.

That afternoon I drove out to the airfield. I was just three flights away from being allowed my first solo flight. It was a beautiful early autumn day, and Bill let me take the controls. We spiralled high on the thermals, then I managed to land the glider safely and smoothly. Bill said he was pleased with my progress and he had high hopes that I would be awarded my pilot's licence in due course.

The next Saturday we played away against Grantly—always a grudge match. Despite being so new to the club, Matt Ridgely had been picked to play scrum half. It was a close game and early in the second half I found myself running the ball up the pitch, heading for the corner flag. From behind, Matt tackled me high round the neck, and I fell to the ground, pole-axed. It was pretty obvious that I was badly hurt: I couldn't feel my legs. I remember Matt's grinning face above me. The ambulance took me to the local hospital from where I was transferred to Stoke Mandeville Spinal Injuries Unit. I spent the next few months trying to get used to the idea that I would never walk again. They introduced me to wheelchair rugby, a game so vicious it is also known as murder ball.

I honestly think it was just as bad for Sheila as it was for me. Matt Ridgely showed a suitable amount of remorse in public, but he was soon sniffing at her door. She visited me at Stoke Mandeville at least twice a week, and I am very glad to say that she has chosen to stick by me, despite my disability. But for how long will she be able to bear it? Matt was given a three match ban for a high tackle—it was decided that it was essentially an accident, albeit with tragic consequences. I decided not to appeal against the decision. He did not visit me in hospital or at home.

Saul McCabe disappeared without a trace: it soon became apparent that he had been using an assumed name. I expect he simply set up somewhere else. I was sorry I couldn't talk to him about my experience on the plane and I spent some time trying to find him, but to no avail. Some people don't want to be found and I suppose we have to respect their wishes.

Sheila has found a course for disabled trainee pilots and I have applied and been accepted. I know she will worry about me taking to the skies again, but she understands that I need to be in the air. I can hear the swifts now, hurtling over the garden. The dreams have come and take me up to where the aeroplane trails criss-cross the sky. Soon I'll be there solo in a light aircraft, my flight path logged, the engine purring. Then I will open the cockpit, unfurl my wings and fly away.

Jetsam

I'm not unique; there are hundreds like me, and others who lost limbs or were killed outright. No matter how alert you were, it could happen at any time. Suicide bombers and improvised explosive devices were almost as common as the flies that continually plagued us. After a while I couldn't relax: I was permanently wired. I'd been shot at by too many insurgents, and shot a few myself. The army offered me counselling, but I didn't take them up on it. I couldn't see how talking to some psychologist would help. I thought I'd snap out of it eventually.

I joined the army because I thought it would make a difference: Queen and Country seemed as good a cause as any. I was sent out to Helmand province in 2008 to join the NATO forces. We were supposed to be training the locals, but soon we were patrolling the area around Camp Bastion, looking out for Taliban gunmen. I enjoyed it at first, and the villagers seemed glad we were there. But as I've said, it began to freak me out. I was there too long.

In 2013 I was medically discharged. I went back to Oxford and held down a job for a while as a security guard, but I wasn't sleeping at night and I dozed off on duty one too many times. After that I was on benefits. I was chucked out of my digs for smoking, and ended up in the hostel.

Alcohol helped with the flashbacks and anxiety and at first I did my drinking alone. Then one evening I stumbled across some like-minded individuals and we met up in back streets or alleys to drink ourselves into a better place. I liked it best when we went to the canal bridge and got pissed under the stars. If it was dry we lay on the ground in the darkness hoping to see a meteorite shower. Occasionally a student pedalled along the tow path, accelerating through us as we jeered. There was no harm in it.

I was the only ex-serviceman of the group, the others were a mixed bunch with problems that had brought them to hostels or homelessness. They say everyone is one bad decision away from the streets. Dave had been chucked out by his missus, Cal was a dyed in the wool alky, and Rob stopped taking his medication. The real alkies were sometimes up for a fight, but mostly they were good blokes, down on their luck—like me.

The hostel is a bit of a dive, but I am fortunate enough to have my own room. I'm seeing a shrink now and I'm applying for jobs. Life is better than it was, but I still can't get the thing I'm going to tell you about out of my head. I haven't talked to anyone about it, not even my shrink.

It started off normally enough. Dave met me outside the Radcliffe Infirmary as usual and we walked along Walton Street to Bargain Booze. Once we'd bought the tins we went down Walton Lane to a yard opposite some garages where we often met the gang. There was no one else there, and Dave said, "All the more for us." We drank three cans of lager each. It didn't touch the sides. Dave started complaining about his ex-wife and, after another can, began to sing—made up stuff. He had quite a good voice, but I was worried the local residents would complain. I'd just managed to shut him up when Cal and Rob arrived. They had brought some more lagers and proceeded to drink them.

The others were pretty legless and talking nonsense to each other when a tall man with grey hair walked into the yard. I recognised the military bearing and was expecting a bollocking for the noise. Instead, he singled me out.

"Would you and one of your friends like to earn some cash? I have a little job I need doing by discreet individuals who don't ask questions."

"How much?" I asked.

"A couple of hundred," he said. "Maybe more later."

"What do you want us to do?"

"Wait until you're sober, then go and see someone. Knock on their door and frighten them a bit. No rough stuff, mind. Just threats. Do you think you could manage that?"

"Yes," I said, almost adding "sir". I was used to following orders. And I couldn't afford to turn down that sort of money. "One hundred up front."

He extracted a wallet from his inside jacket pocket and took out two fifties and a piece of paper with an address on it. I gave one of the fifties to Dave. Cal and Rob had wandered off.

"Where can we find you for the rest of the payment?" I asked.

"I live in a house on Walton Street behind this garage," he pointed to one of the better maintained garages on the lane. "Number 17."

"Should we use your name when we're doing the threatening?"

"You won't need to. They'll know who sent you."

He turned round and was gone. I looked at Dave, who was just sober enough to have understood the conversation.

"Are you up for it, Dave?"

"For a couple of hundred quid I'm up for anything."

The next afternoon Dave met me at the hostel and we walked to Summertown. It was a clear grey day and there was a biting wind. I put my hands in my jacket pockets.

Dave said, "You do the talking, I'll stand around looking tough."

That wasn't difficult: Dave was a very large man with staring eyes and a prematurely lined face from living most of the last few years outdoors.

As we walked into the road I felt nervous, and the flashbacks began. There was one particular incident when children were used as a human shield by a sniper. We had to take out the gunman without injuring the children. A child was hit in the arm. There was blood everywhere and we could hear the screams. I never found out what happened to her.

We stopped outside a large terraced town house with a freshly painted front door and window frames. Whoever lived there was not short of a bob or two. I opened the gate and we walked up the path. I took a deep breath and knocked on the door. We waited for a minute and then I knocked again. The door was opened by a middle-aged woman in a tight-fitting woollen dress. Dave and I looked at each other. Was this really the person we were expected to threaten? I made myself think of the money. Dave put his foot in the door and stared at her.

"What can I do for you gentlemen?" she asked.

"We've been sent by a mutual friend. He's pretty annoyed with you. We're the advance party, they'll be more coming to see you later and they won't be as friendly as us."

She laughed. "Okay, I can guess who you're from. How much has he paid you?"

"All you need to know is that he has a lot of bad things lined up for you if you don't start behaving."

"Tell you what," she said. "How about I give you fifty pounds to ask him to leave me alone. If he doesn't, I'll make life even more difficult for him—trust me, I can do it."

Dave and I looked at each other again. "Okay," said Dave, taking his foot out of the door.

She turned and walked down the hall and disappeared into a room at the end. She returned with five tenners, handed them over and closed the door.

As I shut the gate Dave said, "This is a bit weird, but at least we're making a few quid out of it."

We walked back to Walton Street and rang the bell at Number 17. The tall gent opened the door and ushered us in.

"How did it go?"

"We did as you asked," I said. "She says, leave her alone, or she'll make things even worse for you."

The man laughed hollowly. "You must've got through to her, then." He handed over £150. "I may have another job for you. Come round in a few days' time."

That night Dave and I took Cal and Rob to the Jericho Tavern and we got drunk in comfort. The landlord threw us out before closing time because Dave started singing.

On Friday, Dave and I went to 17 Walton Street. The tall gent showed us into his study. There were books everywhere, piled up on the floor and on shelves.

"She's a witch," he said.

"I wouldn't go that far," said Dave.

"No, I mean she's really a witch, casting spells and the like. She's put a curse on me and everything I do is going wrong."

"She doesn't look like a witch," said Dave. "And she lives in a nice house."

"She makes quite a lot of money in her line of work."

I was dumbfounded. "You think that putting the frighteners on her will help?"

He ran his hand through his hair. "I don't know. I'm at my wit's end. If I don't stop her soon I'll be bankrupt. A business rival paid her to hex me."

"You don't really believe in all that rubbish, do you?"

"I served in many different countries and you know as well as I do that strange things happen. I can think of no other explanation."

"Have you tried paying her to stop?"

"Yes, but she won't budge. It seems there is some kind of honour amongst witches. So I have another job for you. I want you to go round there, but this time it's a charm offensive. You're a good looking chap, see if you can flatter her into lifting the curse. Do whatever you have to."

"How much?"

"Four hundred, but this time it'll be just you."

Dave began to argue but the gent held his ground. It was to be just me and I should go round there as soon as possible.

The next afternoon I knocked at her door and she again took some time to answer. When she finally emerged she was out of breath and looked annoyed, as if she was in the middle of something.

"You again. I told you before . . ."

"I haven't come to threaten you. Won't you let me in? I am house trained." I smiled my best smile.

She sighed and opened the door wide. The room she showed me into was comfortable and elegant, free of magical paraphernalia. She even offered me a cup of coffee. While she was out of the room making it I did a quick recce. There were some books on the paranormal in the bookcase, but nothing about magic or witches. She returned with the coffee.

"So you think you can charm me?" she laughed, handing over the mug.

"It's not like that," I said lamely. "I'm interested in what you do for a living. I hoped you would explain it to me."

"I'm Sandy," she said. "Who are you?"

"Mike," I replied. "I was in the army." I don't know why I said that.

She looked at me for a long time. "Poor thing," she said. "I suspect I couldn't help you much, but I could try."

"That's very kind of you, but I'm really here about . . . I don't know his name."

"He's known as The Colonel. I imagine he paid you to come here? Well, like you, if someone pays me, I feel honour bound to carry out the job."

"He's lost practically everything. Can't you stop it now?"

"I know you won't credit this, but the spell is doubly effective because he believes in it absolutely."

"I'm begging you, Sandy, he seems like a good bloke and it's a crying shame that things are going wrong for him. Can't you think again?"

Sandy gave me another long look, then beckoned me to follow her out into the hall. The room she led me into had the full works; a pentagram on the floor, candles everywhere, wall-paintings of entangled forms. I should've been ready for it, but it was still a bit of a shock.

She leaned over and took hold of my hand. "Don't worry about it too much, Mike. These are just the trappings my clients expect to see. The real work is done elsewhere."

"What do you mean?"

"I can't really explain."

I thought for a moment. "Look, you said you might not be able to help me, but would you try? Alcohol doesn't work any anymore. If you won't help The Colonel, then perhaps you could help me?"

"You'll understand that I have to charge. How much is he paying you?"

"Four hundred."

"That will do."

I didn't really believe in the mumbo jumbo, but it was worth a go. Nothing else seemed to work. Sandy sat me down on a chair, asked me to close my eyes, and ordered me not to open them whatever happened. Then her hands were everywhere, stroking and pulling at my clothes in some kind of massage. Her hands were very strong, almost masculine, and once or twice it felt as if someone else was there with her. I kept my eyes firmly closed and tried to keep the anxiety at bay. She began chanting in a high, loud voice. It made no sense to me, but I felt a slight stirring in the air—I wondered if she was dancing. Then the massage began again. This time it was more personal, and I have to say that I couldn't help but like it. When it was over, she asked me to open my eyes. She was slightly out of breath, and her eyes glittered.

"There you are," she said. "I can't promise it'll be effective, but at least we've tried. As for The Colonel, there's nothing I can do about him. It's too late."

I promised to drop off the £400 in the next few days.

As I walked back to Walton Street, I wondered what I would say to The Colonel. In the event I didn't have to say anything. He saw the look on my face when he opened the door.

He reached into his jacket and handed over the £400.

"Thanks," I said. "Sorry I couldn't help."

I went back to the hostel and read for the rest of the day. Over the next few days I did a lot of walking, out onto Port Meadow and along the canal into the countryside. After a while I noticed that I was having fewer flashbacks. Some of the anxiety had lifted. For the first time in a long while I didn't feel like drinking.

A week or so later I walked over to Summertown. Sandy looked smart in a skirt and twin set. She showed me into the elegant living room and asked me to sit down on one of the armchairs. I held out the money. She took it. "Thank you, Mike. And how are you?"

"I'm having one of my better days."

"Good, that's good. You really shouldn't drink."

"I'm trying,"

"The child is fine," she said.

"What do you mean?"

"The child in Helmand you shot. She's fine."

"How do you know about that?" I stammered.

"She's back at school and there's no major damage."

At the time, I thought Sandy must have looked it up on the internet, but now I'm not so sure. I found nothing about it there myself. She leaned over and stroked my knee. Immediately all the sensations of the week before returned.

"You've had a difficult time. Perhaps things will get better from now on."

Afterwards, I went back to The Colonel and asked if he would employ me as a handyman.

"Alas, no," he said. "One soldier to another, I'm really down on my uppers. Otherwise I'd be happy to. You'll find a job soon enough."

I told him he didn't know what he was talking about. He was taken aback, not used to being shouted at by an ex-private. "You still have this house, while I have nothing. So much for serving my country. Who gives a stuff about me now? After all, I couldn't hack it out there."

I went back to see Sandy every few days—I paid her when I could. Gradually I began to feel better, and stopped drinking. It meant that I couldn't see Dave and Cal and Rob, and for a while that was a problem. Then I began to go to the library—it's warm and dry, and if I read or use a computer none of the librarians bother me. There are a few fellow travellers there and I soon made some friends. I registered at the medical centre and asked a doctor if I could get some help. He found me the psychiatrist, who's a good listener. It kind of works. The pills have kicked in too.

I don't know what to think about the witchcraft, or whether it's just attention from a woman that's making me feel better. She's very good at her job, and who is exploiting who?

I've tried not to have feelings for her, but that's impossible. She has to put up with quite a lot of stick from her neighbours, who don't like her profession, and I've been able to help with that, providing a bit of protection. I suppose if I think of her as the village wise woman, like some I saw in Afghanistan, then it makes more sense.

I've an interview for a security job in Cowley, near the old car factory. If I get it I'll be able to pay Sandy the money I owe her. She says the spells are working, and I can see her for as long as I need to.

Writers' Retreat

Joel applied for the Rawthorpe Award with very low expectations, and so he was extremely surprised to receive a letter from the foundation telling him that he was the recipient of one of the ten writers' bursaries on offer that year. He only filled in the form because Sophie had persuaded him that he should, after he had been complaining that he could no longer find the space or time to write properly in their cramped flat. Alison, their six month old baby, had taken over the tiny spare bedroom which had been his study. This was a major setback for his novel.

The letter explained that he met the award criteria—being an up-and-coming part-time writer with an ongoing project and some publication behind him, who would benefit from a three-week writing retreat in a Scottish country house. He had provided a biography, a CV and a brief outline of his novel, of which he had written the first seven chapters. It was a sort of literary supernatural thriller set in North Yorkshire, where he had lived before meeting Sophie and moving to Oxford for her teaching job. Joel taught adult evening classes at the further education college. In the daytime he mostly looked after Alison, and wrote and planned his lectures while she was asleep. She was sleeping less now and soon would give up her morning nap. Joel had tried not to feel despair at what would happen when Alison became a toddler requiring constant stimulation and supervision. The truth was they needed Sophie's salary, and as he had no formal teaching qualifications he could not justifiably complain about their working or child-care arrangements.

Sophie was wholly positive about the award. "Three weeks of bliss," she said. "You could just sleep through it all if you wanted to." Alison was teething and none of them were getting much rest. "Seriously, Joel, it's great news. They must think you have real potential." She kissed him and they opened a bottle of wine to celebrate. After three glasses, Joel admitted to feeling a warm glow of satisfaction that his talent for writing, such as it was, was being recognised.

Two months later, at the beginning of August, Joel took the train up to London, then caught the east coast express from King's Cross to Edinburgh. He dozed most of the way. At Waverley Station he changed to a local train which eventually dropped him off at Rawthorpe village, where he found a taxi which took him to Rawthorpe House, a large, stone-built Georgian residence set in extensive grounds. It was just as well the award covered his travelling expenses as the house was some miles from the station and the fare, with tip, came to £25. Rawthorpe House was set in a sort of hollow surrounded by high hills and mountains. No other houses or even farm buildings were visible from the house. It was all stunningly beautiful, the wild hills a counterpoint to the manicured gardens and parkland. The photographs on the leaflet he'd been sent did not do the house or its surroundings justice.

It was unclear at which entrance he was supposed to present himself, so after some deliberation he knocked at the rather grand front door. It was opened by a tall, slender man who held out his hand before Joel had a chance to introduce himself.

"Do come in. We've been waiting for you. You are the last to arrive. Of all our award winners you had the farthest to travel. You may leave your bag here."

The interior of the house was just as impressive as the exterior. Exquisite Georgian furniture and paintings lined the long hall. The tall man led Joel to the far end and then opened a door into a large formal dining room full of seated people, the table already set for dinner. Joel felt suddenly overwhelmed as conversations petered out around him. A small, middle-aged woman in a high-necked Chinese dress got up and walked over to him.

"You must be Joel," she said, shaking his hand. "Come and sit down. Now you're here we can serve dinner. I'm sure you must be hungry."

She indicated that he should sit between an elderly man and a young woman with dyed red hair. Joel smiled at them somewhat nervously. The woman in the Chinese dress left the room.

"Are we all award winners?" Joel asked the young woman next to him.

"Yes," she answered. "Not counting Mrs. Howden, of course. She's the supervisor."

"Who is the tall man who showed me in?"

"That's Lord Rawthorpe," said the elderly man. "He allows the foundation to take over his house for three weeks every year. God knows why, but he seems to quite enjoy it."

"I thought he might be the butler or something," Joel said. "It's a pretty amazing place, isn't it?"

Joel had read the information that had been posted to him carefully. He would be seeing his fellow Award winners only at meal times and in the evenings. The rest of his day would be spent in his writers' "cell", where he would be expected to work on his novel. There were ten cells, one for each Award winner. For exercise and fresh air he could walk in the grounds. No other socialising was allowed, and mobile phones were to be switched off.

Mrs. Howden re-entered the room. She wedged the door open behind her.

"Dinner is served," she announced, smiling.

Two young waiters wheeled in trolleys bearing plates of steaming stew and vegetables. There was wine, and the meal, rounded off by fruit trifle, and cheese and biscuits, was excellent. Joel made desultory conversation with Bernard, his elderly neighbour, who was writing a long epic poem. Alex, the young woman with red hair, talked almost exclusively to her other neighbour, a good looking middle aged man with floppy hair. They were discussing various contemporary writers who Joel hadn't read. In fact he found the conversations ranging around him somewhat depressing, his novel seeming pedestrian compared with the projects on which some of the others were working.

At the end of the meal Mrs. Howden stood up.

"We're absolutely delighted to have so many talented writers here with us for the next three weeks. We trust you will make the most of what is, after all, a short period of time, but one which can be of real, lasting benefit to your writing. Many of our previous Award winners have gone on to great things, and there is no reason why that should not be the case for you. So good luck to you all. We will now show you to your rooms and your cells."

Joel's bedroom was small but had a view out onto the front garden and the mountains beyond. There was an en suite shower room. His suitcase had been placed next to the wardrobe. He retrieved his laptop from it and took it with him to his cell, which was tiny, furnished with a desk and chair, an electric socket and a small water dispenser. His name was on the door. There was a lavatory on the other side of the corridor. It seemed that the whole of the first floor had been recently re-modelled—very few original features remained. Nine more cells ranged along the corridor, each with a name plaque on its door.

Night was falling, and Joel felt the need to stretch his legs. He accessed the garden from the conservatory, which ran all the way along the back of the house. Outside on the terrace he came across Alex smoking a cigarette.

"They won't let me smoke inside," she complained, "even though it's really a private house. Lord Rawthorpe doesn't like smoking, apparently."

She joined Joel on his stroll. They stopped by a large fountain. Stone dolphins and fish disported in the bubbling water. Joel thought of Alison, and then realised that it was the first time his daughter had come into his mind all day.

"Are you married?" Alex asked, intruding into his reverie.

"No, actually."

"I'm divorced," she said. "He soon got fed up with me."

Joel thought she didn't look old enough to be married, let alone divorced.

"We're not married," said Joel, "but we have a baby."

"Gosh," said Alex. She took a long drag at her cigarette. "I'm writing a collection of short stories. I don't know if anyone will want to publish them, though. They're experimental. What are you working on?"

Joel explained about his literary thriller. "I've approached a small press that might be interested in it," he said. "But its early days. I'm hoping to make some real progress on it here. So far I've just ploughed on with a first draft, but I've run out of steam." He stopped, aware that he was beginning to mix metaphors.

Alex stubbed out her cigarette on the fountain wall and threw it on the ground. Joel had to stop himself from picking it up. By the time they went back into the conservatory it was dark. Joel said goodnight to Alex and climbed the stairs to his bedroom. As he drew the curtains he glimpsed something pale bounding away from the house towards the parkland—a deer, he thought. It leapt the ha ha with ease. Somewhere, dogs began to bark.

He slept a dreamless sleep, waking late. Breakfast was served in the dining room, where the other award recipients were already tucking into scrambled eggs and smoked salmon. There were pots of freshly brewed coffee and tea. Joel thought that he would have to try not to become accustomed to all his meals being prepared by invisible minions. Gerald, the writer with the floppy hair, asked him about his previously published work—"Just some short stories in small press anthologies," said Joel. It seemed that Gerald had poetry published in *Granta*, but that was some unspecified number of years ago.

Walking out into the garden Joel could see it was a beautiful morning. There was dew on the grass, and birds were singing. The hills were topped with purple flowering heather, the mountains beyond craggy and bare. A gardener was trimming shrubs with secateurs—he waved at Joel, and Joel realised that it was Lord Rawthorpe in corduroy trousers and an old shirt. A large dog—a lurcher or some other kind of crossbreed, lay at his feet, its head resting on its front paws. Joel walked diffidently over to them.

"It's more of a day for being outside than stuck in a cell writing," he observed.

Lord Rawthorpe laughed. "Now, now, Joel, that won't get your novel written. You must make the most of your time here. It will pass quickly enough."

The dog, eyeing Joel, whined quietly.

"Groucho here agrees with you. He's desperate to go on his walk, but he'll have to wait until I've finished dead-heading the roses."

Joel thought again how much Alison would enjoy the dolphin fountain. It was grand, but also joyful and comic.

What must it be like to own a house as large and superb as Rawthorpe? He felt a sudden sharp tug of longing for Sophie. Lord Rawthorpe continued snipping at the rose bushes. Alex walked over to them, puffing on a cigarette. She smiled briefly at Joel then turned to Lord Rawthorpe. Soon they were in animated conversation. Alex, Joel noted, was more confident around Lord Rawthorpe than he could ever hope to be.

"Call me Neville," Lord Rawthorpe was saying. He seemed to have temporarily forgotten his dislike of smoking. Groucho closed his eyes. Joel took the opportunity to slip away.

Ensconced in his cell, Joel opened his laptop. There was no wi-fi to distract him, and the room appeared to be soundproofed. He was soon planning the next few chapters of his novel. The biggest problem was the introduction of the supernatural element. The challenge, as always, was to present it logically, but without losing the shock value. He was envisaging a group of subtle psychic vampires somehow feeding on the main protagonist. The trouble was that he wasn't sure how to write what was essentially horror, subtly. Nevertheless, Joel found himself making a start on chapter eight. The writing went so well that he lost all track of time, and he was so far into it that the knock on his door made him jump.

"Yes?"

The door opened to reveal a rather sheepish looking Alex and Gerald.

"We came to see if your cell is any different to ours," said Alex.

Gerald gave it a cursory once over. "It's exactly the same."

"Are you really managing to work in here?" asked Alex. "It's so pokey and claustrophobic. Not even a window to look out of."

"I don't mind. In fact I was doing quite well," said Joel pointedly.

"It's nearly lunch time," said Gerald. "We're going out for a cigarette. Why don't you come with us?"

According to Joel's watch it was 11:35 am. Lunch wasn't until one o'clock, but he sighed and said, "All right." He saved his work, closed his laptop and followed Gerald and Alex down the stairs and out into the garden. The sun was still shining, although a few fluffy white clouds had gathered on the horizon. Gerald and Alex lit up ostentatiously. Joel looked around the garden—Lord Rawthorpe was no longer in evidence. Alex was giggling at something Gerald had whispered to her.

"He says that you are the only one of us who is normal enough to have procreated. Do you think the rest of us are too selfish or too weird to have children, Joel?"

"I wouldn't like to say."

"How on earth do you manage to write with a baby in the house?" asked Gerald.

The question was rather too close to the bone. "My daughter is a person in her own right, not just an adjunct of me," Joel said, huffily.

"Gosh," said Alex.

"Did you plan to have her, or was she an accident?" asked Gerald cheerfully.

Joel tried not to become angry. "That's really none of your business," he managed to say.

Joel strode off around the parkland. He knew Gerald was trying to rile him—and was showing off in front of Alex. As he walked, he calmed down. It took him almost an hour to complete the full circuit, which meant it must be four or five miles. When he returned, Alex and Gerald were still smoking by the fountain, Alex leaning her head on Gerald's shoulder, her eyes closed. Joel went inside, where preparations for lunch were in train. He met Bernard in the hall, outside the dining room.

"I've made some progress on the poem," Bernard said, "but it could do with being a bit more robust. More vigorous. I should have written it thirty years ago, or when I was your age, Joel."

Two middle aged women came down the stairs together and introduced themselves as Sandra and Billie. They seemed to have been talking about him.

"Alex says you have a baby," said Sandra. "Congratulations! How marvellous."

"How old is she?" asked Billie.

At this point Mrs. Howden appeared and ushered them in for lunch. The meal was just as good as dinner the day before. There were two kinds of soup and a selection of toasted sandwiches, followed by fresh fruit salad and cream. Joel was seated between Billie and Sandra, who asked questions about his home life and his writing. It seemed to Joel less a conversation, more an interrogation, and everyone else was listening in. Alex was sitting opposite him, between Gerald and a man called Simon who didn't seem to speak to anyone. He stared at Joel over his soup bowl.

As soon as Joel finished his lunch he returned to his cell. Chapter eight was a little more recalcitrant than it had been before lunch, but he persevered and it gradually took form. The supernatural element was duly introduced, and he spent the rest of the afternoon writing notes for chapters nine and ten. By five o'clock he'd had enough and went down to sit in the conservatory. There were large cacti, orchids, and other plants he could not name, some of them entwined around the iron pillars that held up the glazed roof. After a few minutes Simon entered from the garden. Joel thought that he and Simon were about the same age, but it was difficult to be sure. Simon wore a bushy beard, an extravagant side parting and thick glasses. He sat down in the chair opposite.

"You may think I'm staring," said Simon, "but in fact I'm so short sighted I have to look at you very carefully to see anything at all. I'm registered as visually impaired."

"That must be . . . difficult for you," said Joel.

"You have a very symmetrical face," said Simon. "I believe that means you are attractive to the opposite sex. You'll have good genes, too. And excellent eyesight, as you don't wear glasses."

Joel could think of nothing to say.

"I'm writing a novel about genetics. I may put you in it."

"But you don't know me!" Joel stammered.

"I'm deadly serious. I need a character who is regarded as 'normal'. You would do nicely."

"For all you know I might have some extraordinary quirk of character, or a mental condition that makes me highly abnormal."

"But you don't, do you? Would you object to me putting you in my novel?"

"I don't know . . . "

Billie and Sandra approached, each carrying a cane chair which they placed either side of Joel.

"Quite a productive afternoon," said Billie.

"Quite," echoed Sandra. "We're both writing historical novels. Mine is about Vikings. A much misunderstood race of people. Billie's is set in the English Civil War."

"I feel sure Joel has Viking ancestry, with that blond hair," said Billie. Is your baby daughter blonde too?"

"She takes after Sophie; she has brown hair."

"Oh well. She still has the Viking ancestry, I suppose."

"Actually, my people were Huguenots, they came from France."

Simon cleared his throat. "It's interesting, isn't it, that we tend to concentrate on one strand of our ancestry. For example, the only thing I know about my antecedents is that I am descended from the prison reformer, Elizabeth Fry."

At dinner, Joel found himself sitting between Graham and Ivor. Graham talked about his currently stalled kitchen-sink-style novel set in a midlands town. Ivor wrote lyric poetry, his last collection having been published some ten years before. Neither asked Joel about his writing, but were content to talk about their own for most of the meal. Sitting next to Ivor was Gavin, who interrupted Graham to ask Joel a question.

"What do you do for kicks? You have to have a bit of time off sometimes, don't you? I go running myself. One man pounding the tarmac."

"I don't have time for anything like that," replied Joel. "I go out with the family if I have any spare time."

Gavin explained that he was writing a novel about the internet age from a Christian perspective.

"Are you a Christian, Joel?"

"No."

"A pity. I imagine you know quite a bit about computers and the internet, though. Would you be able to give me some advice?"

"I really don't think I'm qualified to help. I'm just a computer user with a bit of knowledge—not unlike yourself, I expect."

Gavin proceeded to ask a lot of questions about the history of social media and internet dating which Joel answered as best he could.

"You could try Wikipedia," he said.

"Well, thank you anyway," said Gavin. "I'll make sure you're mentioned on the acknowledgements page."

After dinner the writers returned to the conservatory. Alex and Gerald stood smoking by the door that opened onto the garden. Joel sat next to Billie and Sandra. He wondered whether, because they seemed inseparable they might be a couple, but after some discreet questioning it emerged that they had met for the first time on the train from Edinburgh to Rawthorpe. Billie was small and plump while Sandra towered above her and had a great beak of a nose. Neither of them seemed to have a partner at home, and Joel found himself telling them about Sophie and the tough school she taught in. They were astonished when he explained that he looked after Alison during the daytime.

"It must be rather uncommon," said Billie, "for a *man* to carry out most of the child care."

"You are perhaps a more unusual young man than we had given you credit for," said Sandra.

Joel, who had not thought of it like that before, was more touched by their comments than he cared to admit.

"A baby," said Billie suddenly, "must be tremendously fragile. Are you not sometimes afraid that you might drop her?"

Before Joel could answer, Lord Rawthorpe, dressed in a suit of finely woven woollen cloth, joined them. He sat down opposite Joel. Alex stubbed out her cigarette and took the chair next to him. She reached out and stroked his lapel.

"This is wonderful cloth, Neville. Where does it come from?"

"From Harris. I have enough made each year to make me a new suit. This is the latest."

"It's so beautifully dense and silky."

"The weave and colours are varied each year so no suit is the same."

Every eye in the room was upon them. Lord Rawthorpe began to look faintly uncomfortable as Alex let her fingers linger on the fabric. Eventually she let go and put both hands in her lap. She looked at Joel.

"You've been a dull dog today," she said. "Spending all afternoon in your cell. No one polices us, you know. We can do what we like—within reason," she giggled, catching Gerald's eye. He grinned back at her.

Lord Rawthorpe tut-tutted. "But you're here to further your writing. If Joel is making progress then that is a very good thing."

Gerald laughed. "If you really think that three weeks in a cell is going to turn us into good writers then you are naïve in the extreme."

"Nonsense," said Lord Rawthorpe. "In my experience it can make a significant difference to a writer and their work. I wouldn't bother with all this otherwise. The foundation knows what it is doing. It's a worthy cause and I am rather at a loss to know why you applied for a Rawthorpe Award if you are so out of sympathy with its ethos."

In the silence that followed Bernard cleared his throat.

"Perhaps we shouldn't get hung up on *how* the benefit accrues, but just accept that our time here is short and we should make the most of it in our own way."

All ten award recipients were now in the conservatory, grouped around Lord Rawthorpe. He took out a small camera and stood up.

"I hope you don't mind, but I like to take a photograph of each year's award winners for my records."

They arranged themselves into three rows. Joel stood in the middle, between Gerald and Simon. After Lord Rawthorpe had taken his photograph, Alex produced her phone and asked him to take a similar picture with it. There was a great deal of good natured jostling as more pictures were taken. To Gerald's obvious annoyance, Alex put her arm through Lord Rawthorpe's.

Joel managed to slip away for a brief walk round the garden. Somewhere an owl hooted. He found his thoughts returning to his novel, and felt some excitement as he contemplated the progress he had made. The set up at Rawthorpe House seemed to be working well for him. He was determined to make the most of the next two and a half weeks.

As he approached the ha ha he could see something lying in its ditch—it was the carcass of a faun, its back legs twisted out behind at an unnatural angle. It must have fallen in and broken its spine. Lord Rawthorpe startled Joel by stepping up out of the gloom.

"I can't say I'll mourn it; it's been causing havoc in the garden. I'll have it cleared away in the morning. A quick word, Joel, if I may. It seems that two of our award winners are not using their cells, but are wandering around the house during the day time. As you know, most of the rooms are private and out of bounds, for obvious reasons, mainly because Rawthorpe is my home. You seem a level-headed sort of chap. I wondered if you could have a word with Gerald and Alex—see if you can bring influence to bear. I've tried talking to the young lady, but although she's happy to flirt with me she seems to regard me essentially as some kind of old-fashioned duffer. She may be right about that, but if their behaviour continues then I will have to ask them to leave."

Joel sighed. "I can try, but I don't think they'll listen."

"I'd be awfully grateful," said Lord Rawthorpe.

Joel caught up with Alex and Gerald at lunch the next day. He took them to one side. Gerald was furious.

"He can't chuck us out, surely? It would be bad publicity for the foundation."

Alex stared at Joel. "We're not doing any harm. The family silver is safe."

"Look," said Joel, "why not stick to the grounds and the parts of the house we *are* allowed in. Or just go to your cells and do some bloody writing. That's what we're here for, after all."

"I've writer's block," said Alex sadly. Gerald took her arm and led her out of the dining room.

Joel didn't see them again until just before dinner. Lord Rawthorpe briefly joined the throng waiting outside the dining room and it was noticeable that Alex did not make her usual bee-line towards him. Once they were seated Gerald talked loudly about how successful he had been getting his poetry published in the past. Alex sat next to him in silence and picked at her food. Joel asked if she had managed to overcome her writer's block.

"No," she replied listlessly, "it's worse than ever."

Joel had been sketching out some of the minor characters in his novel. This was new to him, as the short stories he had written previously usually included only three or four characters. He had begun to enjoy the freedom to elaborate afforded by the longer form.

Alex said, "I can see you've had a good day. You don't have to say anything, it's written all over you."

Gerald snorted. "You really are the golden boy, aren't you? Lord Rawthorpe's protégé."

"We're all Lord Rawthorpe's protégés," said Simon. "It's his money that funds the foundation."

"Yes," said Sandra. "His father made his fortune in confectionary. The current Lord Rawthorpe still has a huge income from the businesses set up by his father. The foundation helps him pay less tax but also gives him an opportunity to further good writing, something he's genuinely interested in. He read English at Oxford. He was featured in the *Sunday Times* as Scotland's most eligible bachelor."

"Maybe he's happily single," said Graham.

After dinner Joel spent another hour writing in his cell, then, as dusk fell, strolled around the parkland. As he reached the plantation beyond the southern boundary fence, he heard scrabbling and rustling amongst the trees. Two figures emerged—Alex and Gerald, their clothes askew and dusty.

"Hello, golden boy," said Gerald smugly.

"What are you staring at?" asked Alex, picking a twig out of her hair.

They made towards the house. Joel followed them at a discreet distance.

Joel assumed that Alex and Gerald had found something more satisfying to do with their time than trespass in Lord Rawthorpe's private quarters, because for the next few days he saw little of them, or Lord Rawthorpe. His writing continued to progress well and he was glad he had not been distracted. He was concerned, though, that he was becoming somewhat bogged down in the minutiae of his novel, and was in danger of losing the thread of his main theme. For example, he seemed to be obsessed with describing what people were eating. Also, the minor characters were finding their voices and taking over large sections of the text. Joel didn't know whether to continue with this and see where it might lead, or to stamp it out now and try to write more dialogue for his main character. He also, he realised, badly needed something dramatic to happen.

He had asked Mrs. Howden's permission to ring Sophie the night before. Joel could hardly believe how happy the sound of her voice made him. She and Alison were well and everything was fine, but they were missing him terribly. Alison was going to a temporary child minder in the day time and had settled into the new routine.

"You are eating properly?" asked Sophie. "And getting some sleep?"

At dinner, sitting opposite Ivor and Graham, Joel felt more comfortable answering the inevitable questions, even though Simon, sitting next to him, appeared to be taking notes. Just having spoken to Sophie made him feel far less tense. He was lucky, he realised, to have a family when so many of his fellow award winners were on their own. Alex and Gerald, though, were now very much an item, although he noticed that Alex had begun to look peaky and was still picking at her food.

"So you teach adults in the evenings," said Ivor. "Isn't that rather a thankless task?"

"Not at all," answered Joel. "Most of my students are well motivated, not to say keen."

Sandra asked, "Will you home school your daughter?"

"Oh I don't think so. So long as we can find a good school. We're both English teachers, so she'll need some other specialists to get a rounded education."

After dinner, Lord Rawthorpe was waiting for them in the conservatory. Gerald was holding Alex's arm, and she stayed meekly by his side.

"I think we should play a game," said Gerald. "How about hide-and-seek?"

"Or sardines?" said Ivor.

"I need to have a word with you first," said Lord Rawthorpe. "Something has happened and I'd like to get to the bottom of it. It concerns you, Joel. Your partner Sophie and your child are here. It seems someone telephoned them this morning and told them they were needed here urgently. Sophie has had a very long and tiring journey, and not surprisingly was quite distressed when she arrived. She has spent most of the day thinking that Joel was gravely ill or injured in some way. It was a heartless and cruel thing to do and I'd like whoever did it to have the decency to own up to it now."

There was a long silence.

"Can I see them?" asked Joel.

"Of course you can, once we have finished here," said Lord Rawthorpe. "After you have received an apology from the hoaxer."

There was another uncomfortable silence.

"Very well," said Lord Rawthorpe, "you can rest assured, Joel, that I will find out who did this."

Mrs. Howden ushered Joel into a room off the hall where Sophie and Alison were waiting. Sophie threw her arms around him. Alison was asleep in her push-chair. Sophie had obviously been crying, but rallied now that she had seen him. Joel explained that the hoaxer was not owning up.

"Who would do such a stupid, heartless thing?" she demanded.

"I don't know," he said. "Everyone knows about you and Alison, so any one could have done it. It's easy enough to look up our landline number."

"It was a woman's voice. Lord Rawthorpe is letting us stay for a couple of nights. He is very keen on finding out who the culprit is. Then I'm taking Alison home. I'll not let this spoil your time here. We won't interrupt your writing."

The weather the next day was beautifully warm, and after breakfast Joel showed Sophie and Alison around the grounds. Alison loved the dolphin fountain, clapping her hands and gurgling with pleasure at the spouts of water.

Sophie took Alison to the conservatory while Joel went to work in his cell. He found that he could not concentrate—thoughts about who telephoned Sophie kept intruding. Although he hadn't admitted it to Lord Rawthorpe and Sophie, he had a good idea who it was, but felt no desire to make a fuss and start throwing accusations around. After all, he had absolutely no proof, and could be mistaken.

At lunch, Sophie sat next to him. Mrs. Howden found an antiquated high chair for Alison. All eyes were on Sophie.

"It's very nice to meet you, even under such trying circumstances," said Sandra. "We've heard so much about you."

Billie nodded. "Such a lovely baby! A nice little family. You must be very proud."

Sophie put down her sandwich. "It's difficult to indulge in small talk when I know that at least one of you has maliciously dragged me all the way up here. Have you any idea how that has made me feel?"

The rest of the meal was eaten in silence.

Lord Rawthorpe was waiting for them outside the dining room door.

"I'm sorry to say that no one has come forward. I must say that I am disappointed and disillusioned."

Later in the afternoon Joel left his cell and walked out to the fountain. Alex was there on her own, smoking a cigarette. Joel took a deep breath.

"I'm pretty sure it was you, Alex, who made the hoax call. I'd like to hear you explain why you did it."

Alex snorted. "Oh for God's sake, of course I made the call. You've taken your time working it out."

"What on earth are you talking about?""

"I've saved your bacon."

"What do you mean?"

"All I can say is, go home tomorrow with Sophie and Alison. It's the best thing you can do. Otherwise they'll suck you dry. Just look at me."

It was true that Alex was looking tired and pale.

"I haven't written a word since I've been here." she said.

"Look, Alex, you're obviously not enjoying it. Why don't you ask if you can go home?"

"It's far too late for that."

Alex fell silent as Gerald walked across the lawn towards them. He took Alex's hand and patted it.

"You don't want to listen to her," he said to Joel. "This writer's block thing is getting on her nerves. I, on the other hand, have had an excellent morning. My creative juices are flowing beautifully. It's wonderful to feel so alive."

At lunch the following day Joel found himself accepting second helpings of sandwiches and cake. The atmosphere had improved somewhat, and even Sophie had relaxed enough to chat with Billie and Sandra while she was feeding Alison soup. Joel spent the afternoon reading through the first eight chapters of his novel and making a start on writing the ninth. He was cautiously optimistic about the way it was shaping up, although there was still a lot of writing ahead of him. Sophie was going home in the morning and he found himself wondering how he would find the time to write in the flat once he'd followed her in a couple of weeks' time. He could not imagine how he would feel if he had to give up writing, and found himself thinking of Alex and how miserable her writer's block had made her. He decided that he would not tell Sophie or Lord Rawthorpe that she had admitted making the call—she was clearly suffering from some kind of minor breakdown and he felt sorry for her.

Joel saw Sophie and Alison off at Rawthorpe Station early the next morning. The taxi brought him back to the house and he went straight up the stairs to his cell. From the landing window he glimpsed Alex out in the garden, walking near the ha ha. He worked solidly through the morning, then joined the rest of the writers in the dining room for lunch.

"May I say, Joel," said Graham, "that Sophie is a delightful person."

"And your little girl is so cheerful and lovely," said Billie. "You are a lucky man."

"I know," said Joel.

Gerald cleared his throat. "How's the novel coming along?"

They all looked at Joel expectantly.

"It's progressing," he said.

"Do you think you'll be able to finish it when you get home? With all that baby-minding you have to do?"

Joel smiled. "I'll find a way."

"Are you sure?" asked Gerald. "You seem rather under the thumb of that girlfriend of yours."

Alex, who had been slowly eating her sandwich, looked up at Gerald. "You know," she said, "I'm going off older men." The chair scraped across the floor as she stood up and left the room.

Gerald shrugged his shoulders. "Silly bitch," he said.

When Joel returned to his cell he was almost certain that his laptop was in a slightly different position on the desk than where he had left it. He resolved to password protect his computer every time he left his cell, even though it would be something of an inconvenience.

Taking a break halfway through the afternoon Joel met Lord Rawthorpe and Mrs. Howden by the fountain.

"We were just discussing you, Joel," Mrs. Howden said. "We were saying how we ought to take more care of you. You're one of our more promising Award winners, and you're certainly making the most of your time here."

"I'm awfully sorry that we haven't been able to track down the phone hoaxer," said Lord Rawthorpe. "That sort of behaviour is really beyond the pale. You haven't any more of an idea who it could be?"

"No. Sorry," said Joel.

At dinner that evening the waiting staff hovered around him. The food was as delicious as always and he had second helpings of everything. Alex had not come down to dinner, but the other eight Award winners sat around the table and watched Joel carefully. There were only two more weeks left and if they were to make use of him fully they would have to put the process in operation quickly. Billie, sitting next to Joel, took the initiative and put her hand firmly on his thigh.

House Party

Jamie looked out at the rain, which was falling steadily. The roses hung bedraggled heads and the silent birds, sheltering in the spinney, saved their songs for the re-emergence of the sun. His afternoon walk might have to be postponed, he thought, remembering that he had not brought a raincoat with him, although he was sure he could borrow one. The house seemed well supplied with most things that a guest might need.

It was an afternoon for a game of snooker, or cards—whist or rummy, nothing too demanding. He got up from the chaise-longue. The fire had been lit before lunch, and Jamie didn't know if he should poke it or put some more coal on it. He decided to leave it alone, on the grounds that he understood little about open fires and how to manage them, and was afraid of putting it out. In any case the flames were licking over the coals and the room was pleasantly warm, despite its size. Jamie sank down into an armchair next to the fire.

The door opened and two boys burst in. They trotted over to Jamie.

"We need something to do," said Mike, the smaller one.

Andy nodded. "Mummy said to ask you."

Jamie sighed. "Did she now? Well, what about a good book?" He gestured at the shelves which ranged down one side of the room.

The boys looked at each other. "We have our school books to read," said Mike uncertainly.

Jamie got up. "Come on then, I'll give you a game of knockout whist. You two against me."

He fetched the cards from a table by the door. The boys were jumping up and down with excitement.

"We're going to beat you!" said Andy.

"You can try, but I warn you, I'm playing to win."

As the game progressed, the rain came down harder and rattled against the windows. Andy and Mike were whooping in triumph as their mother opened the door and came in.

"We won, Mummy, we won!" said Mike. The boys ran down to the snooker table and began rolling the balls over the green baize.

Diana pushed strands of wispy blond hair behind her ears. She looked out of the long sash window. "Gavin will be absolutely soaked. Why didn't you go with them, Jamie?"

"Shooting's not my thing."

"What *is* your thing?"

"I don't know," he said, fingering the leather binding on an old book on the shelf. "Reading, perhaps, and keeping your offspring amused."

"Gavin does his best. He plays cricket with them sometimes."

Andy and Mike were chasing each other around the snooker table, sliding on the parquet floor.

Jamie took out the book and opened it. "*The Tenant of Wildfell Hall*. Have you read it?"

"No," said Diana. "I barely have time to read the corn-flakes' packet."

"It's a bit grim. Alcohol is the real villain. The demon drink. Gavin likes a snifter, doesn't he?"

Diana glanced at the boys. "Keep your voice down!"

Jamie put the book back. He pulled out another. "M. R. James. Maybe I should read you a ghost story." He leafed through the volume.

Diana frowned. "I won't have you frightening the boys."

"I'd say they're quite difficult to scare."

"They're not even ten years old!"

Diana expertly shovelled more coal on the fire. Andy and Mike had found the snooker cues and were poking the balls around the table. The rain lashed the windows. From somewhere deep within the house, a bell rang. Jamie and Diana lifted their heads in surprise. After a few seconds the bell rang again.

"The staff have all gone on the shoot," said Diana. "What shall we do?"

Jamie shrugged. "Answer it, I suppose." He had sunk back down into the armchair.

Diana rolled her eyes at him and strode from the room. The boys flopped down in front of the fire, staring into the flames. When Diana returned Jamie could see that something was wrong.

"There's been an accident," she said. "It's not too serious, apparently, but Gavin has been taken to A&E at the local hospital. I'm going to drive there now. Can you look after the boys?"

Jamie signalled his assent. Diana kissed the boys goodbye and left. They were round eyed and solemn.

"What's wrong with Daddy?" asked Mike.

Jamie got up. "Let's see if we can find something nice for you to eat," he said.

He padded along the stone-flagged hall to the kitchen, in the larder of which he discovered a large bottle of cola. Rummaging around in the cupboards he found three glasses and some chocolate bars. When he returned to the games room the boys were sitting silently in front of the fire.

"I'm sure your Daddy will be okay. They'll sort him out at the hospital." He poured out the cola. The boys grabbed the chocolate.

"Mummy doesn't let us eat muck like this," said Andy, peeling open the wrapper.

"I won't tell her," said Jamie.

They finished their drinks and demanded refills. In no time at all they were running around the room again. Jamie looked out of the window. The rain had eased off a little, although water was still dripping from the shrubs and trees in the spinney. Low cloud hung over the hill beyond the garden.

A figure emerged from the spinney, opening the gate and walking over the lawn towards the house. The doorbell rang.

Jamie was unsure how long the boys could be left on their own. "I won't be a minute," he said. The bell rang again as he walked down the hall to the back door. Outside, the waterproofed figure resolved itself into Craddock, the gamekeeper. He wiped his boots on the mat.

"Guns and drink don't mix," Craddock said gruffly. "That silly idiot drank the whole bottle. He's no one to blame but himself."

"How bad is he?"

"Lost a couple of fingers."

Jamie winced.

"It could've been worse," said Craddock, making for the back stairs. "A lot worse. They'll stitch him up and send him back here. I have to fetch some paperwork from the office—I need to fill in some forms. They'll want everything in triplicate."

Once Craddock had gone Jamie returned to the games room. The boys had settled down in front of the fire. Jamie put on a log, then found a game of Snakes and Ladders that none of them had the energy to play. They stared into the fire.

"Do you think Daddy's badly hurt?" asked Andy.

"I'm sure he's okay," said Jamie.

"Shouldn't they be back by now?" asked Mike

It was late afternoon and Jamie assumed the boys would need some more to eat. They hadn't attended the rather grand formal dinners of the last few nights, which were past their bedtime. He went to the kitchen and made marmite sandwiches. They ate them in front of the fire, then fetched their school books. Jamie potted a few snooker balls. By seven o'clock the boys were yawning. Jamie took them upstairs and waited outside while they washed and put on their pyjamas. The house was quiet and cold. He left their bedside lamp switched on.

"We may still be awake when Daddy comes home." said Andy.

"Just concentrate on going to sleep. You'll see him in the morning."

"Goodnight, Jamie," they said in unison.

The fire was barely alight when he returned to the games room. Feeling pleased with his new fire-tending skills he stirred the embers with the poker and shovelled on more coal. Apart from Craddock, the staff had not returned, and were presumably eating their dinner with the shooters at the Blue Boar, where the shoot ball was to be held. Jamie kicked himself for not obtaining Diana's mobile phone number.

The old house creaked. He sank into the armchair and the warmth of the fire soon lulled him into a light doze, the embers glowing beside him. He dreamed he was following a woman through the forest. He could not see her face. She was hunting a giant stag, creeping between the trees clutching her long bow. The dream Jamie looked down at his hand and saw that two of his fingers were missing. Suddenly the stag broke cover and ran a zig-zag path through the forest. The woman let fly an arrow, which pierced the stag in the back of its neck. It fell to the ground . . .

He was woken by the door opening abruptly. It swung into the wall behind with a dull thud. In marched Gavin, closely followed by Diana. Gavin's left hand was heavily bandaged.

"Where are the boys?" Gavin asked, peering around the room.

"I put them to bed," said Jamie.

Diana said, "I'll go and check on them."

Gavin sat on the couch. "This bloody weather is ruining everything. The gun slipped in my hand, it was so wet. Maybe I should sue them."

"It was you that insisted the shoot should go ahead," said Diana. "Craddock wanted to cancel."

Gavin stretched his stocky frame out on the couch. "What have you been doing with yourself all afternoon, Jamie?"

"Oh, you know . . . looking after your children."

"You could get a job as a nanny. Diana'll give you references." He waved his bandaged hand in the air. "What does a man have to do to get a drink around here?"

"Aren't you on painkillers?"

"Be a good fellow and find me a drink, will you. Whisky, if you can."

Jamie rose from his armchair and went to a wall cupboard near the snooker table. Inside were a few bottles of spirits and some tumblers. He poured two fingers of Famous Grouse and gave it to Gavin.

"Is that all I get?" he scoffed.

Diana returned. "The boys are asleep," she said. "Have you told them about Gavin?"

"No," said Jamie. "I thought it was best coming from you."

Diana smiled at him. "You've done a good job, Jamie. Thank you."

Gavin laughed sarcastically. "You see. We'll make a nanny of you yet." He bleated like a goat, and sipped his whisky. "What is it that you do again?" he asked vaguely.

"I've just finished my MA. Victorian literature."

Diana plucked the empty glass from Gavin's fingers. "You've had enough."

"What do you mean?" Gavin spluttered, "You see what kind of treatment I get, Jamie. No consideration at all." He closed his eyes. Within a few seconds he was breathing heavily.

"He's worn out," said Diana quietly. "It was horrible at the hospital."

Jamie stirred the fire. Diana crouched in front of it. "Thanks again for your help with the boys."

"Gavin drinks too much."

"Maybe this'll be a lesson to him."

Jamie gazed down on Diana's slender form. The fire crackled and a piece of coal toppled out onto the hearth. He took the tongs and placed it back on the glowing heap. Outside, it was beginning to get dark.

"Perhaps it will stop raining soon," said Diana.

On the couch Gavin was snoring.

"Do you think we should take him upstairs?" Jamie asked.

"Let's leave him there. I'll find some blankets."

"I'll stay with him," said Jamie.

Diana returned with tartan rugs which they draped carefully over Gavin, then she went upstairs to bed. Jamie sat in the armchair next to the fire—he had retained one of the blankets for himself. The house creaked quietly, and from the hall the grandfather clock chimed the hours. At some point after midnight Gavin stopped snoring. Jamie got up and replaced a rug that had fallen off him. Gavin's breathing was now shallow and somewhat laboured, his bandaged hand twitching by his side. Picking a book at random off the shelves, Jamie settled down to read in the dim light. From time to time he got up to tend the fire.

The clock had not long struck three when the door opened to reveal Diana in a thin summer dressing gown.

"How is he?" she whispered.

"He's been asleep the whole time," answered Jamie.

"Don't you think you should get some sleep?"

"I'm fine. I'm reading."

Diana reached out and stroked Jamie's hair. He caught her hand in his and kissed it: she pulled her hand away. As she left the room, she closed the door quietly behind her.

Jamie slumped down in the chair, his heart racing. Gavin snorted loudly and shifted his position on the couch. Jamie rose and checked on him: he seemed to be still asleep.

In the low light Jamie noticed something lying on the chaise-longue by the window. Thinking that Diana had left a cardigan behind, he went to pick it up, but before he could reach it, the cardigan sat up.

"Love's young dream," said the small man inside it. He had a goatee beard and long fingers, one of which was pointing at Jamie.

Jamie frowned. "Sorry?"

"You're quite the young buck, aren't you?"

"I was comforting her," said Jamie, spluttering. "She's had an awful day."

"So you grabbed a quick kiss while her husband sleeps it off! Tell me, though, just who is hunting who?"

"What's it to do with you?"

"I enjoy the thrill of the chase. I believe she's a few years older."

"So what?"

"And the husband's a drunk."

"He's also a solicitor."

"The thing is, Jamie, do you really want her? And the two boys? I imagine they're part of the package."

"I hadn't thought that far ahead . . ."

Gavin sat up. "Who are you talking to?"

Jamie rubbed his tired eyes. There was no-one on the chaise-longue.

Gavin picked sulkily at his bandage. "I bet they had a good time at the ball." He shivered. Jamie went to the scuttle but it was empty. He picked up a log from the dwindling supply and perched it on top of the hot coals. Flames flickered up the chimney.

Gavin sighed. "I don't mean to drink so much. It just happens."

"Are you seeing someone about it?"

"A shrink, do you mean?"

"A specialist."

"Diana thinks I should. I knew I could count on you to side with her."

Gavin got up and walked unsteadily towards the fire. "To tell the truth I feel a bit groggy. I think the painkillers are wearing off." He hunted in his jacket pocket, drawing out a white cardboard box. He popped two tablets awkwardly from the sheet inside. "These'll sort me out." He swallowed them, and sat down in the armchair opposite Jamie.

Jamie put another log on the fire. "We're running out of fuel."

Gavin picked up the poker. "Why don't you have a kip? I'll keep an eye on the fire. Go on, it's your turn."

Jamie lay down on the couch and covered himself with the rugs. In a surprisingly short amount of time he was asleep, and he didn't wake up until Diana was shaking his shoulder. It was light outside.

"It's stopped raining," she said. "Come and have some breakfast."

The garden still dripped with the remnants of the rain, and low cloud blanketed the hill. Breakfast was in the dining room, where the chafing dishes were full of bacon, sausages, and tomatoes. Jamie helped himself to a mound of food, not having eaten since the marmite sandwiches at tea time. Several other guests were already there, including Andy and Mike.

"Hello, Jamie," said Mike. "Did you know, our Daddy shot his fingers off?"

"He's got a great big bandage," said Andy, "and he can't play cricket."

Diana was eating muesli. Jamie sat down next to her.

"Where's Gavin?"

"Having a lie-down."

Jamie nudged his leg against hers. He felt a welcome pressure in return.

"We could go for a walk this afternoon."

"I may have to look after Gavin."

"Does he need looking after?"

"He's in a tremendous amount of pain. I may have to take him to the doctor. He can't drive."

Diana burst into tears. Andy and Mike stared at her open mouthed.

"Don't worry," said Jamie. "She'll be all right."

Jamie took a shower and changed his clothes. When he came downstairs most of the other guests had congregated in the games room. At some point, the fire had gone out. Andy and Mike sat cross-legged on the carpet playing cards while Diana talked to a tall woman with grey hair. Jamie picked up the book he had been reading and slotted it back on the shelf.

It seemed that a small coach had been hired to take the guests into Durham. Diana, Mike, and Andy were staying behind with Gavin, and Jamie offered to help look after the boys. At ten o'clock the coach arrived and the other guests departed. One of the general staff, a large young man called George, came into the games room and raked out the ashes. He brought in a scuttle of coal and another basket of logs, and lit the fire. Jamie gave him a small tip.

The boys, Jamie and Diana played a rather silly game of snooker, as none of them could remember the rules. Later, Gavin joined them for lunch in the dining room. His bandage was already grey. He found it difficult to eat using only one hand. Much to the amused horror of Andy and Mike, he swore several times. After lunch they moved back into the warmth of the games room. Jamie and Diana played whist against the boys. Gavin sat on the couch, grumbling to himself. Finally he rose and went over to the wall cupboard. He poured himself a large whisky.

"I think you need to see the doctor," said Diana abruptly. "Come on, I'll drive you to the clinic. Jamie will look after the boys."

"Good old Jamie," said Gavin, sipping his whisky. When he had finished it he allowed Diana to lead him out to their car. Jamie heard it accelerate up the drive.

"Let's go for a walk," he said to the boys. "It's ages since we've been outside."

Andy and Mike stood up reluctantly.

"Do we have to?" asked Mike.

"Yes, we do."

They put on wellingtons from the selection in the cloak-room. The grass was still wet, and there were large shallow puddles on the drive. Andy and Mike splashed into them, kicking the water around. Jamie herded them up the drive towards the hill: it was still enveloped in low cloud. The boys enlivened the long trudge by racing each other, leaving Jamie far behind. He sauntered up the bridle path, lost in his own thoughts.

Suddenly he could hear shouts ahead of him. The boys were calling his name. Jamie broke into a run. As he caught up with them he could see through the trees that they were leaning over something on the ground. When he got closer it became apparent that it was the body of a huge stag. The shaft of an arrow stuck out of its neck.

"Is it dead?" asked Mike.

"Of course it is," said Andy, "can't you see the blood?"

The deer was still warm, its coat glistened with moisture from the mist. The tip of one of its antlers had ploughed into the soil.

"It's a beautiful thing," said Jamie. "What a shame someone felt they could kill it."

"Can we have a funeral?" asked Andy. "We had one when our gerbil died."

"I don't have a spade," said Jamie.

They stood in silence for a few minutes, at a loss to know how to mark the stag's passing. In the end Jamie simply took the hand of each boy and led them back down the hill to the house.

Diana and Gavin had just returned from the doctor. Gavin sported a clean bandage and was clutching a new prescription.

"It's to help with the cravings," he told Jamie as the boys took off their wellingtons. "I'm on the waggon."

"Good for you," said Jamie. He went into the games room and put some more coal on the fire. After a few minutes, Diana followed him. She closed the door and pushed the table against it. Then she took him, unresisting, into her arms.

Job Start

Luke found it difficult to sleep during the late summer nights. Half the city seemed to be awake and partying outside until the early hours of the morning. Tonight he was resentful that he was both kept awake and not partying himself, although it was a fact that he could have gone out on the town if he had wanted to.

The house was close to the city centre, one of a street of terraced Victorian houses that had somehow survived the Blitz, and were now rather run down. Most were rented properties, like Luke's. He shared the house with fellow ex-students, Gareth and Johnnie. Gareth had a job in engineering which was something to do with vibrations in wind turbines: Johnnie and Luke were unemployed.

Luke was pretty certain that both his housemates were out: the house was quiet, and Johnnie had a habit of watching television until three or four in the morning, when he wasn't out drinking. Luke threw off the duvet and got up. He stretched—the bed was very uncomfortable and he had been meaning to ask their landlord to replace the mattress. The landlord rarely made an appearance and could only be contacted via the letting agency. Luke pulled on his jeans and went downstairs to the kitchen. Someone had drunk the last of his orange juice so he poured himself a glass of water from the tap. From outside he could hear singing. He found his keys and let himself out of the front door. The singers were a group of men making their way slowly along the street, presumably on their way home. They shouted at Luke in a friendly, inclusive way.

It was warm and muggy. A cloud obscured the moon. Luke sipped his glass of water and looked up at the rapidly lightening sky. Winter seemed far away but he knew that in only a couple of months' time it would be dark by the late afternoons and cold in the evenings. Then, if he was lucky, the revellers would disappear inside until the spring.

From the centre of the city came an orange glow and the hoot of car horns. Two figures turned the corner into the street and Luke saw that it was Gareth and Johnnie.

"You should've come with us," said Johnnie as they drew closer to the house.

"I've got a Job Start interview tomorrow," said Luke. "The plan was to get some sleep."

"You might as well have enjoyed yourself," said Gareth. It was clear that they had drunk a good deal. "Bitter was a pound a pint in town."

They let themselves into the house. Johnnie turned on the television. Gareth went into the kitchen and drank several glasses of water.

"I suppose I'd better go to bed. I've a presentation to make in the morning."

Luke couldn't understand how Gareth held down a responsible job with so little sleep.

Johnnie was laughing at a rerun sitcom as Gareth and Luke went up to bed.

After his interview at the job centre Luke went straight back to the house. He could not afford even to treat himself to a cup of coffee. He went online and began looking for jobs. With his degree in philosophy there was little that would suit him or that he would be suitable for. This had been the theme of the Job Start interview, during which it was suggested that he would have to lower his hopes or lose his welfare benefits. It was made clear that he was expected to work anywhere that would have him.

Or he could go home to Sussex, where his parents would grudgingly accept him, but where there were even fewer job opportunities. There he could walk in the wild woods, and hear the birds sing, and roam along the deep narrow lanes under the trees, and drink local beer in country pubs—until his parents tired of him or his benefits were withdrawn. Luke felt as if he was expected to make important decisions about his future without being aware of all the facts. Johnnie and Gareth seemed able to bumble along quite happily: Johnnie had managed to stay out of work for over a year without anyone taking away his benefits.

After lunch Luke set off on one of his long afternoon walks. He made his way out into the leafy suburbs where large houses stood in substantial grounds. He walked on to where the countryside began, climbed a tree and read his book for a while. The heat was palpable and closed in around him. He swigged water from a plastic bottle and dozed through to the evening. On the way back home he bought fish and chips and ate them from the paper in the street.

At home Johnnie was watching television in the sitting room. Gareth had yet to return from work. Luke fetched two cans of lager from the kitchen and gave one to Johnnie. Johnnie had read French at university—he was a year older than Luke.

"When Gareth gets back we're going to the pub. Do you want to come?"

"I might," answered Luke. "I'm pretty skint, though."

Johnnie returned his attention to the television.

"I could do with a few tips on how not to have to take a job."

"Oh, I don't know," replied Johnnie. "I just say what they want to hear and they seem to leave me alone. It's sort of a game. You have to learn how to play it."

Johnnie gulped down the lager. They heard Gareth let himself in through the front door.

"How did the presentation go?" asked Johnnie.

"Oh, fine," said Gareth diffidently. "They liked it. They're taking me to Berlin next week."

"Cool," said Johnnie.

In the pub the three of them sipped their beer. The Friday night crowd was beginning to trickle in, and the landlady, an old friend, shouted at them from the bar.

"All right, my lovely boys?"

They nodded cheerily. Gareth put his glass down on the table.

"I'm going to be working away over the next few months. After Berlin they're sending me to Minnesota."

"Are you keeping on your room?" asked Johnnie.

"I'll still be paying my rent," Gareth assured him.

Luke sighed. "So the gang of three is breaking up. I suppose it had to happen at some point." He took a gulp of beer.

"We'd better get pissed then," said Johnnie. He went to the bar to order three more pints.

"What are you going to do with yourself?" asked Gareth once Johnnie had gone.

Luke laughed. "I suppose I'll have to take a job. I lack Johnnie's skills as a layabout."

Johnnie returned with the beer. The pub was so crowded it was difficult to have a conversation. The pints slipped down quickly and Gareth got up to fetch some more.

On Monday Luke received an email from his Job Start coordinator informing him that he would be expected to attend a job interview the next day. It was at a private house in the suburbs and the job on offer was part-time general handyman and gardener. Luke knew nothing about gardening but it was made clear in the email that he would be assessed on whether or not he made a good impression with the interviewer. The would-be employers were a Mr. and Mrs. Hardy.

Gareth had left the house early to catch his flight to Berlin. Johnnie was still in bed. Luke lay on the sofa contemplating the cracks in the ceiling and fantasising about how his charm would help him become the adopted son and heir of wealthy, childless Mr. and Mrs. Hardy. In the fantasy, he would eventually inherit their large Edwardian villa and never have to work again.

The next day Luke walked out to Fallside, the suburb where the Hardys lived. He was surprised to find himself turning into a cul-de-sac of modern brick detached houses, each with a tidy area of lawn and flower beds at the front. Number 15 was in the middle on the north side of the road. The doorbell was answered by a middle-aged man in a business suit—there was a child's pushchair in the hall.

"Oh hullo," he said. "You must be Luke. Come on in."

Luke stepped over a teddy bear. Somewhere, children were singing.

"I'm Simon Hardy. My wife is going to interview you. She'll be down in a minute. I'm just off to work. Come into the kitchen and have a cup of tea."

The kitchen had an Aga and was pleasantly warm and comfortable. Children's paintings covered the walls. Luke sipped his tea.

"We're looking for someone who can work flexible hours and is versatile," said Simon. "Sioned has a lot on her plate with the children, and she works from home. She can't be expected to manage the garden and chores as well."

Luke nodded.

"Do you like children, Luke?"

Luke swallowed. "Oh yes. Not that I've had a lot to do with them. I was one once, of course."

Simon raised his eyebrows. "Some contact with the children would be unavoidable. You do realise that?"

"Um, yes."

"And that's all right, is it? You'll have to have all the proper checks and everything."

"How many children are there?"

"Well, there's Ella, who's four-and-a-half, and the twins. They're two."

"Right," said Luke.

There was a pause in the conversation. A woman put her head around the door and then came in.

"Hello, Luke. I'm Sioned."

Sioned was some years younger than her husband. She extended her hand for Luke to shake.

"Well, you seem strong," she said. "Are you a gardener?"

"I'm not very knowledgeable, but I am good at following instructions." This was the answer Luke had practiced on his way to the interview.

"And Simon has explained about the children?"

"Yes."

"Then I think you're hired!"

Simon grasped Luke's hand and shook it.

"Well done, you've passed."

Luke blinked a few times, then managed to say "Thank you very much."

Luke began working for the Hardys the next week. Ella, the eldest child, was at school, and Sioned put the twins down for their afternoon nap before coming out into the back garden to tell Luke what to do. It was very hot. He mowed the lawn, then began to weed the path. The garden was long and surprisingly large for so modern a house. There was a swing near some apple trees. Sioned sat on it for a while before returning to the house to work.

"I'm a food and wine journalist," she told Luke in her lilting Welsh voice, the swing rocking back and forwards, her toes pointing out in front of her. "I specialise in British cuisine." Her skirt brushed the grass.

It was a long path and there were many weeds growing between the flags. Luke levered out each unwanted plant and threw it into a bucket. The garden had a slightly neglected look, but even he could see that it would not take much to put it back in good order. He couldn't imagine that he would be needed for more than a few hours each week.

Later, Sioned brought the twins out to play. They were a boy and a girl, Bryn and Sukie, and they toddled around the garden together. Both showed some interest in Luke and his task, crouching down to examine the weeds. Sioned sat on the swing and watched them. The twins began singing in a high-pitched warble, achieving a curious kind of harmony. The sound was not unpleasant but Sioned laughed and put her fingers in her ears.

Simon Hardy arrived home, bringing Ella with him. He changed out of his business suit and joined his family and Luke in the garden. Luke had nearly finished weeding the path.

"Splendid job, Luke," said Simon, kissing Sioned on the top of her head and putting an arm around her shoulders. "Did you finish your article, darling?"

"As near as damn it," said Sioned.

"My wife's been finding it hard to complete things since the twins were born. She needs a bit more help around the place, that's all."

Sioned got off the swing. "I'm perfectly all right," she said. "Don't listen to Simon."

Ella ran up to look at what Luke was doing. "Daddy, he's cutting out all the plants!"

"That's what we want him to do. He's making everything neat and tidy."

"But I like the little plants!"

"There are plenty of flowers for you to like."

Once more the twins began their eerie singing. Both Ella and Sioned put their fingers in their ears. Simon said, "Can't you stop them making that infernal racket? There's something wrong with them, I'm sure."

Two days later Luke returned to the Hardys. Sioned asked him to weed the flower beds. This was a more difficult task as he was not always aware of what was a flower or a weed. They agreed that Sioned would come out to the garden every quarter of an hour or so to point out the plants he could remove.

The system worked well. It was still very warm and Sioned seemed listless. At three o'clock she made them both a cup of tea and they sat on the terrace to drink it.

"Where in Wales do you come from?" asked Luke.

"Gwent," replied Sioned, "a place called Caerleon, near the border with England."

"Do you miss your homeland? It must be different here."

"I miss the green hills on summer nights, and the singing of the birds . . . "

After they had drunk their tea Sioned left with the twins to collect Ella from school. Luke lay down on the grass and gave himself up to the sun.

Luke got into the rhythm of working three afternoons each week for the Hardys. As soon as he had tidied the garden, the weather broke and the autumn storms began. Sioned found some indoor jobs for him, including putting up shelves in the twins' bedroom and fitting a new carpet in the hall. While Sioned worked in her study, Bryn and Sukie would sit close to Luke and sing their curious songs. As the twins grew used to him, Sioned left them more in his care. In truth he did not mind, because they were a self-sufficient pair and needed little input from him. Ella was harder work, but she was at school for most of the afternoon and so he had less time with her.

One day, after a few weeks, Simon came home early. It soon became evident that he was in a foul temper: he slammed the bedroom door when he went up to change and shouted at Sioned, even though he knew Luke and his children would hear. Ella began wailing, and Luke, who had been mending a kitchen cupboard, put his arm around the little girl to comfort her. Simon came into the room in time to see this and lost his temper, accusing Luke of worming his way into the affections of his wife and children.

"You want me to care for your family don't you?" said Luke, trying to keep calm. "That's what you pay me for."

Simon went out in the car, screeching tyres on the drive. Sioned came down the stairs to the kitchen, and picked up Ella.

"He's lost his job," she said. "And we're mortgaged up to the hilt. My measly earnings won't cover it. I'm sorry, Luke, we're going to have to let you go."

Luke couldn't help it, he put his arms around Sioned and Ella. Upstairs, the twins began to sing. Then he saw Sioned's shocked face and let go. He fetched his coat from the hall and left by the back door.

"Bad luck," said Johnnie. "I know you were on a cushy little number there. Wait till Gareth comes back next week and we'll drown our sorrows. He'll be loaded. I'm completely broke."

Later in the week Luke took one of his long walks to the suburbs, but it was cold and he could not recapture the old magic. He had not meant to, but he walked to Fallside—Simon's car was in the drive of Number 15. Somehow Luke found the courage to ring the bell. Simon answered, and had the good grace to look ashamed.

"Luke, I behaved very badly towards you and I apologise. Come in out of the rain. The family would love to see you."

Luke found himself in the living room, where the children were playing. They rushed over and grabbed him round the legs.

"Luke! Luke!"

"Is Sioned here?" he asked.

"She's upstairs writing an article. She's our breadwinner now."

Simon went to the bottom of the stairs and called his wife to come down.

Sioned looked pale. She would not meet Luke's eye.

"I wanted to say that I would gladly work for you for nothing," said Luke, looking at Sioned.

Simon shifted uncomfortably. "That's not really going to happen. We have our pride. Besides, I'm able to do the chores for the time being. Until I find another job."

Luke was silent. The twins began their unearthly singing. Simon told them to stop.

Gareth returned from Minnesota early in November with presents of duty free spirits for Johnnie and Luke, and, after they had helped Gareth clean his room and the communal rooms of the house (it was a bit of a mess), he took them both out to dinner. Johnnie had at last been unable to avoid taking a part time job waiting tables at a café in town. Luke was working in a library on a voluntary basis. They went to an Italian restaurant in the city centre where they drank three bottles of red wine. Gareth regaled them with tales of his time in the States, although he had mostly been working. Then they went to see a band. When Luke finally went home to bed, his ears were ringing, and in his drunken state he thought he could hear the singing of the twins.

At the library Luke spent most of his time shelving returned books. He found the work congenial because he could sometimes read a few pages, and then borrow the books that seemed the most interesting. Once or twice he found one whose pages sang to him.

After a few weeks Luke received a phone call from Simon Hardy. He said that he had found a new job and they would like to employ him again on the same basis as before. Luke felt that he should say no, or play hard to get, but instead he said, "I'd love to." He arranged to go to the house that afternoon.

Sioned and the children let him in. They all went into the kitchen, which was as warm and cheerful as he remembered it. It was the half-term holiday and Ella pointed out some of her new drawings on the wall. The twins clung to Luke's legs and sang. Sioned said, "Could you rake up the leaves in the back garden? Simon thinks they look a mess."

The leaves from the beech and apples trees were wet but easy to scrape into piles. He transferred the leaf piles to the large compost heap in the far corner of the garden. It took him barely half an hour.

Back inside, Sioned made them tea. Luke said, "I've been discovering some Welsh writers in the library I'm working in."

Sioned went to the window and looked out at the garden. Darkness would soon be upon them.

"You've made a good job of the leaves . . . "

"Your voice is a song," said Luke.

Sioned could not find the courage to turn around.

Productivity

The scent of lilac wafted across the garden. Melissa raised her head and watched as the zephyr lifted the skirts of the columbines and ruffled the blowsy peonies. The murmur of the bees did its best to lull her back into lethargy, but it was time to rouse herself: she had been lying in the sun too long.

Even though she had raised the sash windows and wedged open the back door, the house was as hot as the garden. Melissa poured herself another glass of wine and, eating her meal at the kitchen table, looked outside. The breeze had abated and the flowers basked in the warmth of the evening. It was beautiful, she thought; at its best. The long June evenings meant she could work on the garden once the sun had lost its strength.

Martin appeared at the open door.

"You're not out in the sunshine?"

"I've been in the garden all afternoon."

"It looks good. For a purely decorative garden, that is." Martin stepped into the kitchen and drummed his fingers on the work surface. "You know, you have room for a decent vegetable patch. And a few fruit bushes. It wouldn't take much to dig it over. I'll give you a hand."

"Thanks, but I like it the way it is."

"That's all very well, but there are other considerations." Martin picked up an unopened letter from a pile on the dresser and held it up to the light. "It'll be 'Dig for Victory' again before we know it. Then you won't have any choice. If you want fresh vegetables you'll have to grow them yourself." The letter was addressed to Greg. He put it down with the others.

On the TV news were more stories about the shortages, and the next day Melissa, stopping off at the supermarket on her way home from work, found empty shelves in many of the aisles. After unpacking her shopping she walked round to Martin's house—he was drinking coffee in the conservatory with Olla. Martin greeted Melissa as if he had not seen her the evening before.

"How are you?"

"I'm well, Martin. I wanted to ask about the shortages."

Olla stirred her coffee. "Don't get him started on that subject."

"If you really think about it," said Martin, "there's every reason to believe they'll last for some time."

Olla asked Melissa if she wanted a cup of coffee and stalked off to the kitchen to make it.

"Don't mind her," said Martin. "In Russia when she was growing up they were often short of food."

"And they managed somehow."

"Yes."

Olla returned with the coffee and a plate of biscuits. Melissa sipped the hot coffee.

"So I can't persuade you to grow vegetables?" asked Martin.

Olla said, "I can remember when you and Greg moved in. Such a lovely young couple. So many plans."

Martin frowned at her.

Melissa sighed. "Greg had plans of his own."

"You're better off without him," said Martin.

"He is very handsome," said Olla. "The girls like him."

"Never mind about that," said Martin crossly. "How can we help Melissa?"

"I'm not sure Melissa needs any help," said Olla. "She is happy with her garden the way it is."

⁂

The evening was as warm and still as the day had been. Melissa went out and weeded beneath the roses. Everything seemed to have grown several centimetres overnight. The first of the oriental poppies were now coming into flower, each bud case bursting open and falling to the ground. Fern fronds unfurled themselves from their fist-like cores. When she had finished weeding Melissa unwound the hosepipe and watered the flowerbeds. The heady scent of lilac permeated across from the tree by the wall.

If only it would stay the way it was, before the most attractive flowers went over and their bright foliage faded to brown. Every day since Greg had gone Melissa had tended the garden they had planned together, had seen it in all its incarnations, but this time in June was the best. She lay on the grass and looked up at the columbines, their young stems yearning towards the sky. She fell asleep and awoke when it was dark, the ground cool and damp beneath her, the stars pulsing above.

⁂

Melissa cut back the daffodils, tulips, and bluebells that had flowered in the spring. The fine weather continued, and most evenings after work she was able to sit out in the garden. One evening she was reading in her deckchair when Olla appeared at the gate. Olla sat and chatted about people they knew. There was a pause, and she caught Melissa's eye.

"I wanted to ask you about Martin. I know he comes round here. Oh, don't worry . . . he feels protective, I think, since Greg left. Does he talk to you?"

"About what?"

"I don't know. About rationing. About the shortages."

"Sometimes."

"You see he's stopped talking to me."

"He gives the impression that he knows a lot more than he's prepared to admit."

"It's his job. While he's selling the farmers insurance he talks with them."

"He thinks I should dig up my garden and grow potatoes. But I'm growing flowers for the bees. There are still bees in my garden."

Olla stood up and strolled over to a tall white lily, its sickly sweet scent assailed her as she looked into the star-shaped flower. Several small beetles crawled around inside. "Your garden is beautiful, but I think Martin is right." she said. "He is talking about getting some chickens."

At the end of August the fine weather broke. Thunder-storms drenched Melissa's flowers and Martin's carefully hoed vegetable beds. Melissa studied her garden from the kitchen window. Bedraggled foliage bowed to the ground, rainwater streamed down the path and the water butt over-flowed in front of the shed. Before she could go out to fix it Martin appeared with some cauliflowers and courgettes. He carefully removed his muddy wellington boots at the door.

"I'm storing apples in the spare room," he said. "I've been reading up on the subject. We're making jam and chutney too."

Melissa was finding it increasingly hard to track down nice food. "When it stops raining, I'll tidy my garden for the winter."

"They say it's best to do it in the spring. You leave it a mess over the winter for the wildlife to enjoy."

So Melissa left the garden to its own devices. Gradually, over the autumn the foliage flopped into pulpy brown clumps. It rained almost continually from November to March. There were widespread floods. Melissa waited until early February, then began to clear up the mess. Snowdrops were already raising their heads through the leaf litter. She moved the dead vegetation onto the compost heap, and after a couple of days' work the garden was tidy once more, ready for the flourish of spring growth. The daffodils and tulips brought colour in March and April, and as May turned to June the garden was again at its best.

Olla weeded and watered her garden while Martin was at work. Melissa went over to buy eggs, but this time, Olla would only let her have two. Melissa tried not to look disappointed. Olla said, "Chicken food is hard to find. We're feeding them mainly on scraps and they're not laying the way they used to."

Melissa mowed her lawn, then lay down on the grass. The roses were in bloom, as were the columbines, cornflowers, and poppies, but the insect hum was muted. There were fewer bees this year.

In the evening Melissa weeded between the poppies. Martin let himself through the gate and flopped down on the grass beside her.

"You have been very stubborn about your garden. I can bring you some vegetables in a few weeks—beans and courgettes—but I don't want money for them. We're bartering now—eggs for sugar for the chutney and jam, for instance." He leaned over until his mouth was close to her ear. "You need to offer me something in return," he whispered.

Melissa stood up. "I'll work on your garden in the evenings. Olla is looking tired. I'll help her."

She could see that Martin was angry. He got up and put his hand on her arm. She stepped back, her fists clenched. "Leave me alone."

Martin laughed at her. "You think you're safe in your little piece of paradise." He stalked off.

Every weekday evening Melissa spent an hour or so working in Martin and Olla's garden, weeding and hoeing. Olla often helped, and the two women worked together, side by side. Martin was employed for long hours and was rarely home before Melissa had left. At the end of each week Olla presented Melissa with some produce—strawberries and raspberries, runner beans and cauliflowers, courgettes and potatoes. Melissa carefully washed the vegetables and fruit and stored them in her fridge. They augmented the rationed staples—meat, bread, rice and pasta—that she was still able to buy from the supermarket. One evening she picked a selection of flowers from her garden and took them round to Olla. Olla smiled and said, "Thank you, Melissa, they're beautiful," and put them in a vase on the mantelpiece.

Later that evening Martin eyed the flowers as if they were some kind of ghastly affront. "Useless," he said. "We won't be offering her anything in return."

"Martin!" Olla cried. "Melissa brought the flowers as a gift!"

"I'm working every hour just to scratch a living, while she swans round and does a little weeding and gets her hands on our food."

"She's a real help," said Olla. "And I like her company."

Martin put down his briefcase. Olla realised he was very weary.

"The ministry has changed the subsidy arrangements. The farmers are asking my advice."

"But that's not your job!" said Olla.

Martin sighed. "We're expected to pull together."

In July it rained. The vegetables in Martin and Olla's garden grew more profusely than ever. Melissa's flowers bloomed as the sun shone between the showers. Martin had been seconded from his insurance firm into the ministry, where he was advising on crop production. There were worries about the wheat harvest—a wet August would be a catastrophe. Olla and Melissa were carrying out most of the work in his garden.

Melissa found that she had less time to tend her own garden. The tall plants were left after flowering and weeds sprung up among the flowers. One Saturday Melissa spent most of the sweltering day in Martin and Olla's vegetable patch, then Olla said: "Now we will work in your garden, Melissa."

Together they dug out the weeds and cut back the straggling plants. Melissa mowed the lawn. Within a few hours the garden was back to its best. Melissa threw her arms around Olla's neck.

"Thank you! Oh, thank you!"

In the evening Melissa, exhausted, sank into her deckchair. A blackbird hopped across the lawn, pecking at worm casts. Overhead, the swifts flew in a long formation, screaming over the garden as they dipped to catch the midges. Thunderclouds loomed, and rain began to fall, conjuring the musty scent of newly moistened earth from the ground. Melissa sat in her deckchair, letting the raindrops wet her face. The shower was soon over.

Thunder rumbled in the distance, and the metallic tang of electricity hung in the air. Melissa could picture the combine harvesters in the broad fields, racing to bring the harvest home.

Martin let himself through the gate.

"It's official! The minister agreed to my suggestion. All gardens are to be made productive. You'll have to dig this over before spring or else pay a fine."

"Then I'll pay the fine," said Melissa.

"You'll have to do it eventually," he said. "You will get your garden back when the crisis is over."

"There'll always be a crisis," said Melissa. "I'd like to keep my little piece of paradise."

"And what will Greg say?" asked Martin. "Surely he still owns half the property? I'd like to speak to him about it."

Melissa felt the old fear return. "He's not easy to get hold of."

"You'll have a phone number for him? A forwarding address? You must need to talk to him from time to time."

Olla walked over the grass. "I asked you not to bother Melissa this evening."

"She doesn't know how to contact Greg."

"Well he's the one that left. It's up to him to let her know where he is."

"It's been two years, surely she should be over it by now!"

Melissa put her hands over her ears. "Stop it! Please!"

Olla stroked Melissa's hair. "We will help you," she said.

The rain came down in earnest, and they raced into the kitchen. Olla and Martin sat at the table while Melissa filled and switched on the kettle. Martin said "I can hire a rotavator. We'll cut back the vegetation first, then set the machine on it. It'll take less time than you imagine."

Melissa thought carefully. "All right, but I'd like to keep a small part of the garden as it is. Just to remind me how it used to be. I'll mark it out before we start."

Martin nodded his assent.

When they had gone Melissa found some string and canes and marked out a rectangular area of flower bed in front of the shed. It wasn't the prettiest part of the garden, but it was the most productive.

The flowers grew tallest there.

Voluntary Work

The drop-in group met every Wednesday morning at the St. Francis Centre. Sometimes there were activities—painting a picture or learning something new on the computer—but mostly it was a social event. Once a month the group went out on a trip in a minibus. Val, the volunteer group co-ordinator and driver, was in charge, and there was also a volunteer helper whose job it was to push Carol's wheelchair. Everyone else was able to walk, after a fashion, though most only with the aid of a stick.

For the last few weeks the volunteer helper had been Bruce, who was taking a year out before going to university. Pushing Carol's wheelchair over rough ground was a difficult business. Bruce was also expected to feed Carol at lunchtimes. At the Centre the meal was cooked by volunteers, but on trips out the group went to a café or a restaurant, often one associated with the attraction they were visiting. Favourite haunts included an ice cream parlour on a dairy farm with pet animals, and the street market of a local town. They tended to visit the same places often, as some attractions were more willing than others to accommodate a largish group of disabled people, many of whom had had strokes and could not communicate well. Bruce, however, had other ideas. One Wednesday he brought in a brochure from the local scenic railway.

"They have a steam train and everything!" he enthused. "And they positively encourage disabled passengers. We can definitely take Carol."

Carol smiled and nodded her head several times.

"See," said Bruce, "Carol likes the idea."

Val sighed. "It is quite expensive, though, and it would be a long day. Perhaps we should put it to a vote."

The vote was overwhelmingly in favour of the trip, and so two weeks later Bruce found himself manoeuvring Carol's wheelchair out of the minibus, up a ramp and into an old-fashioned railway carriage. The huge old engine had arrived at the station billowing smoke and steam and the male members of the group spent several minutes admiring it. Val had been assured by the railway company that the group could have a carriage to themselves, which was essential as Carol's wheelchair would partially block the corridor. It took nearly ten minutes to get everyone on board, and they were only just installed when the whistle blew and the train began to steam slowly out of the station.

Val stood up and conducted a head count.

"You all need to stay in your seats while the train is in motion," she said. "And we're going to the end of the line. We're not getting off at any of the smaller stations."

Les whispered something to Derek and they both laughed. Val frowned. The train was clattering through the outskirts of the town. Carol's eyes danced with excitement.

"You wait until we *really* get going!" Bruce said. She smiled and nodded.

"Where are we eating?" asked Derek.

"We've organised a real treat," said Val. "We're having a picnic on the train!"

"Sandwiches, you mean," said Les. Derek laughed.

"It'll be fun," said Val firmly.

"Is there a bar?" asked Malcolm.

Bruce said, "We'll have a look later, when we stop at a station."

"Look," said Val, "we're out in the countryside."

They could hear the staccato chuff-chuff-chuff of the engine as the train picked up speed. Outside were rolling fields enclosed by dry stone walls beside small clumps of woodland. Most of the group were looking out of the windows. There were sheep everywhere.

"I bet you can't count them all," said Bruce to Carol.

After a few minutes the train decelerated and shuddered to a halt at a small station. Old carriages and decaying rolling stock littered the sidings alongside the track. Malcolm, Derek and Les stood up, and Bruce led them along the corridor.

Val said, "We'll have a choice of soft drinks served with our lunch."

No one else seemed to want to find the bar. In fact the rest of the group were sitting in silence. Val wondered whether she should initiate some kind of community singing, but just then the train began to move again, and a tall man in a uniform entered the carriage.

"Tickets, please."

Val handed over a sheaf of tickets. The man was looking at Carol's chair.

"I'm not sure you can keep that there."

"Where else could it go?" said Val. "You're not putting it in the guard's van."

"It might come to that," the man said.

Malcolm, Les and Derek returned, carrying plastic pint glasses brimming with beer. Bruce followed behind.

The ticket collector said, "I'll go and make enquiries."

"You can't move Carol, she's our fairy godmother," Bruce said.

Carol rolled her eyes and smiled. The ticket collector, who had not looked at her until now, turned tail and left the carriage. Low cheers broke out.

"Carol: one, petty officialdom: nil," said Bruce.

The undulating hills soon gave way to moorland. They were in a mini-wilderness, with only purple flowering heather and bracken in view. The engine worked hard as it pulled the carriages up an incline.

Les said, "They promised us a carriage to ourselves, and that includes Carol. If they want to move her we'll ask for our money back."

"It may not be as simple as that," said Val.

"Why not?" asked Derek, sipping his pint. "If they promised."

"Come on, Carol, girl," said Malcolm. "Time for some of your magic."

Carol closed her eyes.

"That's it," said Derek.

Carol opened her eyes.

"Is it done?" asked Les.

Carol nodded.

The carriage door slid open and a trolley full of food was pushed in by a young man in a catering uniform. "Lunch is served," he boomed. The sandwiches and drinks were handed round, and general munching ensued. Bruce fed tiny portions of sandwich to Carol. When they had finished, the young man returned and cleared away the wrappers and bottles.

"You see," said Val, "I told you it would be fun."

All of a sudden the engine shuddered and squealed to a stop. Out of the window they could see men in orange dayglow jackets walking along the length of the train. After several minutes Grace said, "It's broken down. We're stuck in the middle of nowhere."

"We could be here all night," said Les, winking at Derek.

"Don't be silly," said Val. "If there's really a problem, they can send another engine."

The ticket collector entered the carriage. "There's nothing to worry about. We just have to locate the problem and fix it, then we should be on our way."

"They haven't a clue what's wrong," said Malcolm under his breath. Several members of the group were looking downhearted.

Derek said, "It's another one for Carol."

"You must stop this nonsense," said Val. "It's not helping her. You're giving her ideas."

"Rubbish," said Les. "It's only a bit of fun."

Carol closed her eyes. Bruce said, "I suppose Carol wouldn't do it if she didn't like it."

After a few minutes the ticket collector put his head around the door. "It's all sorted. We're off again."

"There you are!" said Malcolm. "She's done it again."

Twenty minutes later the train pulled into the station at the end of the line. It was in a small town in which there were a number of tea rooms catering for passengers and other tourists. The group took some time to disembark, and Bruce calculated that they had less than an hour before they needed to catch the return train. Val, who had carried out some online research, led the party to one of the larger cafés. They found several free tables at the back of the dining area, next to the lavatories, and it took some time before the waitress came over to take their orders for tea and cake, and even longer for the food and drink to arrive. Val had to hurry them along, and once they had paid there were only a few minutes before the train would be leaving the station.

Val ran on ahead to try to make sure the train didn't leave without them. Carol's wheelchair clattered over the uneven pavement. Some of the slower walkers were falling behind.

"Make the train wait, Carol," said Les. "We don't want to be stuck in this dump."

Once again, Carol closed her eyes. When they reached the platform the train was still there. Bruce asked the guard for the ramp and pushed Carol back up into their carriage.

No one seemed to be suggesting that she should move to the guard's van. The rest of the group settled themselves in their seats and the train began to move.

Once more they were scything through the countryside, and several members of the group settled into sleep. Malcolm and Grace poked their heads out of the high carriage windows, watching the engine disgorge steam and smoke, and the pistons drive the wheels.

"Watch out for tunnels," said Les.

"Yes, please do be careful," said Val, who was feeling rather sleepy herself.

Carol was looking out of the window, smiling.

"Do you like the train?" Bruce asked. Carol nodded fiercely.

Derek said. "Do another of your spells. Go on, Carol, I dare you. Get up and walk away from that bloody chair." He laughed heartily.

Carol thought of the nights she had flown out of the window of the care home, the town lights glinting beneath her, the children out on the town in the early hours she had kept an eye on, the families she had woken when a burglary was ensuing. But most of all she thought of the freedom of the wide sky and the power of her own limbs to dance and swerve through the air.

The train halted at a small station and the ticket collector and one of the maintenance men entered the carriage. The ticket collector was holding a small posy of heather which he held out to Carol. Bruce took it for her.

"We thought you might like to smell the heather. It's only in flower for a few days each year."

Carol blinked slowly three times. "She says 'thank you'," said Bruce.

"We're volunteers too," said the maintenance man. "This whole railway runs on voluntary work. We wanted to thank you for your help."

Bruce held the posy up to Carol's nose. "Carol is a remarkable person," he said. Carol closed her eyes and sniffed the sweet heather.

"She is also a forgiving one," said the ticket collector. He touched Bruce's hand. "You'll find a way of looking after her."

Messages

The message is hand written on a scrap of paper stuffed in an envelope. It reads:

"Are you blind to the truth?"

I study the shaky capital A, attempting to winkle out some clue about the sender, then I stow it in the filing drawer with the others.

The messages are delivered when I'm out. They lie on the doormat waiting for me in their cheap manila envelopes, the flap tucked in rather than stuck down. I have come to expect them once a week or so, and if a week is missed out, I feel strangely bereft. They are not obscene or threatening, only puzzling and odd.

The writer is going to some trouble: I almost admire his persistence. I find myself wondering if it isn't a case of mistaken identity—for one thing, my name is not written on the envelopes. Perhaps he's putting them through the wrong letterbox.

Previous messages have included "You know what you must do", "You cannot run away", and "Give me a sign that you have understood".

The most likely explanation is that I have a stalker, one who takes care not to reveal himself. All I know is that he can spell, and that his hand shakes when he writes. Although the messages are obscure, they are an attempt to mould my behaviour. I'm not doing whatever it is he wants me to. What would I have to do to make him stop?

I close the curtains and lie on my sofa. Am I the only one to whom he is sending messages? It's a subtle form of intimidation, and efficient—they are troublingly enigmatic. Perhaps there are other recipients who, like me, are wondering what can be done.

Many people would say that I should talk to someone—a trusted colleague or friend. It might be unkind, though, to place the burden on another's shoulders. In any case they would only tell me to go to the police, who would point out the lack of identifying evidence and send me on my way.

Like most men I have not led an entirely blameless life. There have been certain incidents, some murky encounters. That was in the past. Many of the people involved are incapacitated or dead—I am longer lived and hardier than most of them. I may have inconvenienced a few people: my night club employed some dubious characters—a former bare-knuckle boxer and an ex-thief amongst them. I needed people who knew how to take care of themselves, keep others in line. I wanted my customers to have a good time without worrying about troublemakers.

The messages hint at some kind of secret from the past. Most people have secrets; I am sure I am no different from anyone else in that respect, only I am better at keeping them. It is likely that the messages are some random prank—children, perhaps, bored on their way home from school. If that is the case then I have nothing to fear.

I lock up and walk down to the high street. The shops are bedecked with multi-coloured light displays and gaudy Christmas tat. Darkness falls quickly. I find myself going into a café and buying a cup of coffee, even though I could've drunk one at home. The café is full of harassed parents with squawking children. I drink my coffee quickly and move on to the only pub that is open all day. Four pints later and I am in no mood to be pleasant to anyone, so I stagger home. It is raining and cold, and when I get back I take out the messages (I have kept them in order) and read them again.

❧

He has dwindled in his dotage, the old soak, although he clings to a semblance of a life. There is no point to his existence except for him to acknowledge what he has done. It is only for that that I hope he lives a little longer.

I am sick of his complacent face, the blurriness when he gets drunk, the fighting talk. Why should he enjoy himself when I have been destroyed?

There is a score to settle.

He knows who I am and what he must do, even if he has yet to admit it to himself.

❧

I fall asleep on the living-room floor and wake in the morning to see the messages spewed over the carpet. I pick them up and sort them roughly into order, then I go into the kitchen and splash cold water on my face. My head pounds, my body aches. I eat a rudimentary breakfast.

Today is the day for cleaning the house. There are few rooms so it doesn't take long. Twenty years ago I lived in a large house and employed a cleaner who came twice a week. I lost most of my money when the night club was shut down, but had enough cash salted away to buy this small house on the edge of town. It suffices.

After I have dusted and vacuumed and cleaned the bathroom I put on my coat and walk to the supermarket. It's busy and full of "Christmas Fayre", even though it is only the beginning of December. Outside it's snowing again,

143

wet stuff that does not accumulate but lingers in a layer of slush on the pavements. I place provisions in my basket and pay at the checkout.

On my return home I find another manila envelope on the mat. It has come sooner than expected. I put down my shopping bags and open the flap. Inside is the usual torn off piece of paper. This time the message reads:

"Don't make me come for you."

There it is, for the first time: a hint of menace. I put the message in my pocket (I will think about it later) and make myself a cup of tea. Tonight, in the pub, I am meeting an old friend from my days in hotel management. After my nightclub was shut down I worked as a manager in various enterprises, including a second hand car dealership and a restaurant. Since I retired I am often bored; the pub provides a certain amount of companionship, but I am still not used to filling vast expanses of time.

Bob is already in the pub when I arrive. He has put on more weight and is almost spherical. In the old days he was a fit, svelte young man. I have managed to keep myself trim. I offer him another drink and he asks for a pint of bitter.

When we have our drinks in front of us I tell Bob about the messages. I show him the latest. He laughs.

"Someone's little joke."

"But whose?" I say. "They're getting weirder."

"If you're worried, go to the police."

"They'll not help me."

"Maybe there's a serial stalker out there. It could be a woman."

"I don't think so."

"Why not? You had plenty of them in the old days. You were quite the lad."

"Not anymore."

Bob took a sip of his beer. "I'll put out a few feelers if you like."

Bob is a Mason. I think about it, then nod my assent.

The conversation turns to other things and we drink a few more pints. Eventually the landlord asks us to leave and we part outside the door. It is cold and crisp and I am not entirely sober. A chill wind whistles past my ears.

I doubt that Bob will be able to help me. I'm not sure that anyone can.

In his heart he knows who hounds him, but he will not admit it to himself. There are so many things that he is responsible for, but only one that warrants the treatment he is receiving. Surely he can see that, and knows what he must do.

Today I am tired. I slept badly and when I dozed off my head was full of dreams. In one I watched a dolphin disporting in a small pool. It writhed and leapt, desperate for deeper, wilder water. I heard my dead mother's voice say, "Come on, the water's lovely!" I felt compelled to jump in, but hesitated . . . My dreams are usually anodyne. There were others, but I cannot remember them.

I make myself breakfast. Today I must telephone my sister in Glasgow. She likes to keep in touch. I don't think I will speak to her about the messages, she would fuss so. She thinks she is looking after me from afar, reminding me to go to the dentist and when to send birthday cards to our cousins in America. I have told Bob; that is enough for now. A useful indulgence. When I phone her she does nothing but complain: about the weather, her husband, the government: I find an excuse to cut the call short.

Walking is my only exercise. Wrapped up against the cold I stroll around the perimeter of the park. There are few people about: a father, mother and two boys playing football, a toddler and grandmother feeding the ducks. The sky is an iron grey, the trees skeletons, the pond a sheet of tinted glass. I walk three circuits and then go home.

There is another envelope waiting for me.

It reads, "Time is running out."

I screw up the scrap of paper and throw it in the bin. Then I take out the other messages from the filing drawer and set fire to them in the grate. I watch the brief burst of flame, then I pick the latest message out of the bin and throw it into the fire. Soon, all that's left is a pile of grey ash. When it has cooled I brush it up and tip it into the outside bin. There will be no more intimidation. Future messages will be destroyed and I shall not read them first.

Time to play a different game. He's a hard man but I will break him.

His arrogance and wilful ignorance amaze me. Is it possible that he has forgotten? In which case he is even more hideous and unfeeling than I had thought.

I will win, however long it takes.

I am lying in bed and the stairs are creaking as if someone is walking up them. I climb out of bed and switch on the light: I step out onto the landing but there is nothing to be seen.

I experience some difficulty in getting back to sleep. In the morning I am tired. As I make breakfast I find the kitchen has been subtly rearranged. The toaster is further along the counter; the knives are in the wrong compartment in the drawer. Either I have become forgetful, or someone is playing a trick on me. Who is able to get into my house? I check my spare keys are still on the hook, then I ring a locksmith and arrange to have the locks changed.

At lunchtime I escape to the pub. Bob is sitting in the corner, nursing a pint. I buy myself one and sit next to him. The place is deserted.

"I was going to ring you," Bob says. "I made a few enquiries. The police have no knowledge of a stalker in the town. They will have a look at your messages, though, as a favour to me."

"I'm afraid that won't be possible. I did the sensible thing and burnt them."

"That's a pity," says Bob. "There could've been DNA."

I realise that I look foolish, but somehow I know that there was no trace of anything incriminating on the messages or the envelopes.

In the evening I settle down in front of the television. Soon I fall asleep. A terrible howling wakes me. I open the back door and the decibels increase. There is something puzzling about the sound; it seems to repeat itself, as if it is recorded and playing over and over again. I shut the door and eventually the dog, if that's what it is, quietens down to the occasional whimper.

At night, a myriad tiny noises, like a plague of beetles, steal my sleep. In my restlessness I am aware of every sound. They may be the usual noises of the house wrought loud to my over-sensitive ears. At last I fall into a dream-laden sleep. I am back in the night club; the pleasure-filled evenings merging one into the other, hard work keeping it afloat beneath the swan-like glide upon the surface. We could do little about the drugs, and most of the time we did not want to. In the dream I am happy to see the young people enjoying themselves. Then the lights go on, and the girls begin to scream. It's another police raid, and the young people's former joy seems tawdry and cheap—the girls have sweaty, mascara ravaged faces and the boys rumpled clothes.

I wake to the drip, drip, drip of the bathroom tap. It has been left on all night and there is not enough hot water for a shower. I wash as well as I can in the sink. In the kitchen a mug has fallen off the draining board and smashed on the floor. I clear it up and throw the pieces in the bin. A fall of soot from the chimney has dirtied the living room carpet. I take out the hoover and vacuum up the mess.

I do not want to be in the house so I go out for a walk. People are using the park as a short cut to get to work. I walk around the perimeter three times, then stand by the lake, my reflection a rippling blur. The sky is dark and it may snow again. Will there be a message waiting for me when I get home? I do not want to go back to find out.

I sit in a café and drink coffee. I have not brought a book, so I watch the people pass by; the happy, smiley ones, the busy arrogance of others.

Something is coming. I can feel it in my bones.

He is rattled—his house is no longer his own. Soon he will run out of time and the reckoning will begin.

Eventually I steel myself to go home. There is no message, but the bathroom tap is dripping again. I tighten it—there is nothing wrong with the washer. In the afternoon the locksmith arrives, a cheerful young man who quickly removes the old locks from the front and back doors and fits sophisticated replacements. I pay him and twist the new keys onto my keyring. When I go upstairs I find my duvet scrunched up on the floor. The window is closed and locked. I am outraged that someone has been in my bedroom, but now the locks have been changed it shouldn't happen again.

I switch on the lights in every room.

When I go to bed I leave my bedside light on. I sleep a dreamless sleep. All seems well when I get up: it is quiet and an inspection of each room yields no unpleasant surprises. Outside, a hoar frost covers the ground, and when the sun rises over the horizon the sky is revealed as a clear wintry blue. I decide to go out early, locking the doors with my new keys. The high street is deserted except for joggers and a young woman who lets herself into a greeting cards shop. I walk to the park—there is ice around the edge of the pond and the ducks sit on frozen mud under the trees.

As I turn, the ground begins violently to shake. Terrified, I fling myself to the ground—a jogger, running past, asks if I am all right. I get up and find that all is still. The few people around me do not seem perturbed, in fact they carry on their activities—walking, running, talking—as if nothing has happened. I feel foolish, brush the frost off my trousers and carry on.

As the sun rises the sky turns a fiery orange. An icy wind whips up and dry leaves skitter across the path. A gust blasts me in the face and I experience an involuntary intake of breath. Everyone else seems to have gone home or taken shelter: I am blown off the path onto the still frosted grass. As the wind buffets me further from the path I grab a tree trunk and hold on as the storm howls around me, the branches above my head whipping and bucking so much that I am afraid they will break off and fall on my head.

The wind drops. The sky returns to blue, the trees are as still as stones. The storm has passed and I walk swiftly into town. It is still early but some shops are open. I go into the newsagents and look through the local newspaper—there are no reports of strange disturbances in the town. The proprietor is staring at me so I buy the paper and throw it in the litter bin outside. I go to the pub but the door is locked. I bang on it for some minutes: no one comes, so I buy beer in the supermarket.

At home, I inspect each room before I settle down to drink. All is quiet and tidy. I tug open the ring pull on the can and think about the last two messages: about what has been happening to me. A thought forms in my mind, one I would rather wasn't there.

I swig the beer, then open another can.

He is beginning to understand what this is about. We must turn the screw before he drinks himself into a stupor.

How can it be that? I took care that no one knew about it.

The windows begin to rattle—the whole house shakes. Lumps of plaster fall from the ceiling.

It was a response to the circumstances, an act of defence. I would have done anything to keep the club open. It was one of many things . . .

I did it myself to make sure that it was done properly. She was always hanging around, refusing to go away. It took a while for me to work out that she was informing on us to our rivals. At that time the police were raiding us every other week. I have no regrets over it. It was a struggle for survival.

I'm not a squeamish person—I drove out to the countryside, dug a hole and buried her. Her family reported her missing, but the fuss soon died away. She was by then an addict: the police decided she'd run away to London or gone off with some man. When their inquiries trailed off, I got on with fighting the war.

The rattling stops. The house settles into silence.

I have acknowledged it. Will he leave me alone?

I open another beer and switch on the television. It's the usual gameshow, followed by the news.

I watch as an aerial shot of a small wood appears on the screen. There is a tent in one corner, protected by police tape. The reporter is saying:

" . . . a dog walker has found skeletal human remains near the village. A police spokesperson said that it is too early to identify the victim. Forensic experts are working at the scene."

❧

She is free! She is free! At last, we are free!

Entitlement

Alicia had never met an "honourable" before. Chris was the youngest son of the Duke of Northampton, and therefore The Honourable Christopher Cathcart, a title to be used only, he explained, in the third person. Being Honourable did not stop Chris from stealing college crockery and, at the May Ball, several crates of white wine that had been left unguarded in the bar. Chris also stole paperbacks from Blackwell's, and just about anything he could get away with. Alicia's unease at this behaviour—in fact it was more than unease—made her feel very prudish and middle class. He and his fellow Old Etonians didn't seem to think about it much, they just did it. In some ways she envied them their élan.

Alicia suspected that Chris regarded their relationship in much the same cavalier spirit. He seemed very affectionate when they were alone, but with his friends it was if she were vaguely irrelevant. Her girlfriends, many of whom, like her, had made it to Oxford by being the most ambitious and clever students at their local comprehensive, were in awe of Chris, who was tall and could be very charming when it suited him. Alicia wasn't sure where the liaison was headed, but she had decided it was worth going along for the ride.

It was unlike any relationship she'd been in before. For one thing they rarely had a conversation about anything, and he always paid the bills. It was as if money was of little importance to Chris, although wealth was obviously what made his family tick. He seldom talked about his parents, and he seemed uninterested in Alicia's.

The college fellows held a series of dinners throughout the year to which undergraduates were sometimes invited. Alicia, being a promising student of modern languages, received an invitation to her tutor David Fulking's dinner, to be held a few days after the May Ball in the dining hall adjoining his rooms. The rooms on this staircase, in the south western corner of the main quad, had a reputation for being haunted, although no supernatural activity had been reported in recent years. The stories amounted to little more than sudden chills and slammed doors, nothing, perhaps, that could not be experienced from time to time in most Oxford colleges.

Chris had also been invited to the dinner. There were twenty of them ranged around the long oak table: Chris was seated at one end, well away from Alicia. At his end of the table bread rolls were being thrown. David Fulking gazed fondly at the assembled diners, his gold-rimmed spectacles glinting in the candlelight. Chris and friends had started on the wine, in fact had already demanded refills from the waiting staff. Fulking did not seem inclined to call order or impose any kind of more gentlemanly conduct on his unruly guests. He made a little speech about the Rosetta Stone, and then the rather indifferent food was served.

It soon became apparent that Chris was drunk: he had probably been drinking before the dinner. He complained loudly about the soup, then shouted out "Alicia," and waved down the table at her.

"That's a fine frock you're wearing. I'll have the pleasure of taking it off later!"

There was a burst of laughter round the table. Alicia, flushed with anger, chewed stoically through the dinner. Chris continued to play up to his equally drunk friends, who had resumed throwing food around. They were all members of a dining club that specialised in trashing restaurants, so she supposed this was normal behaviour for them. Alicia had worked as a part time waitress while still at school and could not help but feel sorry for the staff who would have to clean up afterwards.

At the end of the dinner coffee and mints were served. David Fulking made another little speech about how hard work usually pays off, and then everyone was getting up to leave. Chris advanced across the room towards Alicia. She put out her hand and stopped him before he could take her arm.

"You're drunk, Chris, and a little bit obnoxious."

"Oh, come on old thing, cut a chap some slack."

"You always talk like that when you're drunk."

"Like what?"

A little crowd of Chris's friends had gathered around them. There were raucous cries of encouragement.

"You'd better go back to your rooms and sober up."

Chris put on his most persuasive voice. "Won't you come with me?"

"No."

He let out a bark of laughter, then swept off with his friends. Everyone else in the room was looking at Alicia. She held her head high and strode out.

On the staircase it was incredibly cold: Alicia shivered in her summer dress. David Fulking was following her down.

"Here we go!" he said. A door slammed somewhere. "The lady is angry."

"What lady?"

"Don't you know? The ghost is supposed to be a woman of the town wronged by one of the fellows. When she announced that she was expecting his child, the fellow strangled her in these rooms. He got away with it. Every so often she becomes angry and haunts us. Can't blame the poor thing really."

"What a horrible story," said Alicia.

"It's more than a story."

"Do you believe in the ghost?"

"Oh, I think so. Why not? What other explanation is there?"

Alicia went to her room, which was in the modern block at the rear of the college. As she undressed she tried to think rationally about Chris. He had behaved so appallingly at the dinner and yet no one else seemed to care very much. It was almost as if it was expected of him. She was sure that if she had behaved like that she would've been asked to leave, or at least not invited again. Chris was hardly a model student so it seemed odd that he had been invited at all. She supposed it was "The Honourable" thing rearing its head again. Chris would always be invited.

The next morning Alicia bumped into Chris in the refectory. He was looking decidedly the worse for wear. They sat next to each other, eating their bacon and eggs. From time to time Chris groaned.

"I can't keep apologising," he said.

"And I can't keep forgiving you," said Alicia.

They looked at each other for a long time.

"Listen," said Chris, "the long vac is nearly with us and I have to go home to help Pa with the estate. We only have a few more days, so let's enjoy them. Let's hire a punt."

He hadn't invited her to meet Pa, she noticed. And Chris wasn't even inheriting the estate. His elder brother Henry was. She sighed.

"Okay, a punt it is."

He brought a hamper and a bottle of champagne. Chris, it turned out, was very good at steering the punt, and they raced along with the current, overtaking several more mediocrely crewed craft. After a while they moored on the river bank, opened the champagne and demolished the contents of the hamper. Chris pulled her down into the shallow bottom of the boat. A few minutes later, when Alicia struggled up for air, a small woman in an old-fashioned dress seemed to be waving at her from the meadow. Alicia, a little bit tipsy from the champagne, waved back. The woman waved harder, and then was gone.

"Who are you waving at?" asked Chris, pulling her back down into the punt.

The next day he took her out to lunch at the Taj Mahal on the High. He was on best behaviour, carefully polite with the staff and charming with her. They even talked about possibly going away to Italy in August, although it was all a bit vague. Chris's family had a villa in Tuscany, but it seemed that it was often lent to friends. He would have to find out when it was free. Meeting his family still did not seem to be happening, and Alicia could not bring herself to ask him about it. She would be going home to her mother in Market Harborough: Chris said he might be too busy to visit. After lunch, they ended up back in his rooms. He had been drinking heavily and Alicia let him sleep it off. Chris's rooms were away from the main quad, in the oldest part of the college. He had a sitting room to himself, as well as a comfortable bedroom. Most undergraduates had to share sitting rooms, or resided in poky single rooms in the modern block, like Alicia. Chris snored his way through to the evening. Alicia sat in a chair and watched him carefully to make sure he didn't choke.

The next day was their last together before Alicia went home. Chris had arranged to meet her in the Turf Tavern, which was where they had first met. Alicia had been with a mixed group of freshers and Chris was at the bar, on his own for once, drinking whisky and sodas. It was Alicia's round and as she stood next to him, trying to remember what everyone wanted to drink, Chris said, "Why don't you ditch your friends and come and have a drink with me."

Alicia's mother drove down to collect her. She was in a hurry to get back as she was going out with a new boyfriend in the evening. Alicia found her bedroom was exactly as it had been when she had left home at the end of the Easter vacation. Her mother seemed pleased to have her back. Alicia messaged some of her old school friends and arranged to meet up one evening in the week. By the end of the next day she had talked her way into a temporary job waitressing at the restaurant she had worked in when she was at school. She slipped back into her old comfortable life, and sometimes remembered to think about Chris.

Tasked with finding savings in the cattle feed budget, Chris found himself thinking about Alicia. She cared for him—even if she was a bit censorious at times. He would like to hang on to her, and he supposed it was about time he knuckled down to some college work. He wanted to come out of it all with a half-decent degree.

Back in Oxford David Fulking was witnessing some strange goings-on. Unlike many fellows he lived in his rooms and was staying in them during the long vacation. The staircase was glacially cold and he often heard footsteps running up and down at odd times of the day or night. When he went out to look, there was no one there. Doors constantly slammed. He began to keep a diary so that he had a record of the manifestations. David had been privy to many supernatural goings on all over Oxford—it was one of his hobbies to investigate such phenomena and he had agreed to take these rooms, which many other fellows had turned down, because of his interest. So far, nothing had manifested itself inside his rooms, and he was grateful for that. Something, though, must have set off all this activity.

Chris hadn't heard from Alicia in two weeks and was beginning to feel anxious. This was an unusual sensation for him. In the end he rang her mobile, which she answered, though she sounded somewhat distracted. She explained that she was at work.

"I just wanted to hear your voice," said Chris.

"Well now you've heard it."

"Are we still on for Tuscany? The villa is free for the first two weeks of August."

"I should be able to make it. Will it be just us?"

Chris swallowed hard. "I thought so. Is that okay with you?"

Alicia laughed. "Chris, you almost sound nervous. Of course it's okay with me."

"Only, my brother Henry might show up at some point."

"It'll be nice to meet him."

Alicia had earned enough money waitressing to pay for her own flight to Florence. Chris hired a car at the airport and they drove to the villa, which turned out to be palatial, if rather lacking in furnishings. It had a swimming pool, and a couple, Signor and Signora Capello, resident in the grounds who cleaned, gardened, and generally looked after the place. Alicia insisted on having her own bedroom—the villa was not exactly short of them—although as it turned out she spent most nights in Chris's room. It was blisteringly hot, and they did little for the first few days except lounge around the pool reading. They also took the odd stroll in the grounds, which were extensive and laid mainly to grass. Signor Capello had a sit-on mower which buzzed around most mornings. In the evenings they went to the bar in the village. Alicia had never seen Chris drink so little. He was on the waggon, he said, although he indulged in the odd glass of red in the bar.

On the fifth day, when they were sitting in the shade on the verandah, a Mercedes turned in to the drive and parked around the back.

"That'll be Henry," said Chris.

A taller, better looking version of Chris walked around the side of the villa.

"Hello," he said. "You must be Alicia."

Henry walked up to her, bent down and kissed her on the cheek.

"Hi," said Chris. "Are you on your own?"

"I am for a few days, then Charles and the gang are coming over from Florence. I see you've made yourselves at home."

"Naturally," said Chris. "I squared it with Pa before we came."

"Did you tell him about Alicia?" asked Henry.

There was an uncomfortable silence. Alicia sat forward on the sun lounger.

"So I'm your dirty little secret?" she asked Chris archly.

"No . . . it was just easier . . . oh, for heaven's sake!"

Henry laughed. "A lovers' tiff already. What a great holiday this is going to be."

Signor Capello appeared from the side of the villa carrying three large leather bags. He took them inside.

"Travelling light?" asked Chris.

"Capello likes having something to do. Unlike some."

Chris stretched out on his sun lounger. "We're relaxing. It's nice to be out of the hurly-burly. Why don't you join us?"

Henry fetched a sun lounger from beside the pool and placed it next to Alicia's.

"I can keep an eye on you two from here."

After lunch Henry disappeared into his bedroom. Chris said, "I haven't told you much about my family, have I?"

"Practically nothing."

"When Pa dies Henry cops the lot. Piers and I have trust funds, of course, but essentially that's how it works. Henry has always been the apple of Pa's eye. He's everything you might want in a son and heir. I'm the spare and Piers is the afterthought. Piers is still at Eton."

"What do you want to do with your life, Chris?"

"I don't really have to do anything if I don't want to."

"You mean you'll have enough to live on without finding a job?"

"Probably. It depends a bit. I might want to work, though."

"What would you do?"

"I'm not sure. Something in the City?"

Alicia regarded him thoughtfully. "What does your mother think of all this?"

"She and Pa separated when Piers went to prep school."

"Don't you see her?"

"From time to time. Not very often. She has a new life now."

Henry sauntered out in a bright pair of shorts. Chris raised his eyebrows in mock horror.

"You'll frighten the natives."

"Can't see many of those around."

Alicia said, "Let's drive out somewhere this evening."

"Good idea," said Henry.

They dozed the rest of the afternoon away.

When the day was beginning to cool they climbed into the Mercedes and Henry drove them out into the countryside. Chris sat in the front passenger seat while Alicia lounged in the back. The two men talked quietly leaving Alicia free to look out of the window at the scenery. Eventually they stopped in a hillside town and ate at a small restaurant which specialised in seafood dishes. While they were eating Alicia was puzzled by the appearance on the other side of the town square of a woman in old-fashioned dress who seemed to be waving at her. When Alicia eventually stood up to approach her the woman had disappeared. Chris laughed at Alicia when she explained.

"Waving at the locals again. You've been drinking too much of the vino."

Back at the villa Signora Capello had turned down the beds, although not the one in Alicia's room. Alicia decided that it was time to exercise some independence and sleep in her own bed, but all that happened was that she and Chris ended up in her room. Alicia got up to use the bathroom during the night and found that the villa had grown very cold. One of the bedroom doors slammed, and she remembered David Fulking and his college staircase.

Early the next morning Henry and Chris insisted on playing a game of tennis on the asphalt court below the swimming pool. Feeling somewhat superfluous, Alicia pretended to read her book. The brothers squabbled more or less good naturedly over the game. Before it became too hot to play they managed a set, which Chris won six to four.

Henry took them out to lunch at the bar in the village. Chris had started drinking again. Alicia could feel, but not fully understand, the tension between the two brothers. It seemed that Charles and his friends would be arriving in two days' time. Chris was annoyed—he thought he had use of the villa for a fortnight. Henry brushed off his concerns.

"Nonsense, there's room for all of us. Alicia doesn't mind sharing, do you Alicia?"

Chris was knocking back the wine at an alarming rate.

When they returned to the villa Chris went to lie down in his room. Alicia sat on the verandah with her book and was soon joined by Henry. He moved a sun lounger over until it was next to hers, then he lay down and closed his eyes.

"Are you a little gold-digger, Alicia, or do you really care about Christopher?"

Alicia swallowed her indignation. "Of course I care about him!"

"Well if you do then maybe you could have a go at stopping all this thieving he's indulging in."

"How do you know about that?"

"We have our spies. It would only take one conviction to mess up any future career he might have. Pa has asked me to have a word."

"With me?"

"Yes. I know Chris doesn't want you to meet the family, but we do know about you."

"I'm not sure there is much I can do to stop him. Why don't you have a word with his friends?"

"We can't do that."

Alicia thought for a moment, then rolled her eyes. "Because they're your pals."

"I see you're not entirely devoid of brains."

Chris appeared later on, after Henry had driven off somewhere. He apologised for drinking too much at lunch time and promised, without prompting, that he would try to curtail his alcohol consumption for the rest of the holiday.

"I've been thinking. Why don't we move on to Rome before Charles and Co. arrive? We've had a good laze here. Time for some city action. We can rent an apartment on the internet."

"That's a great idea," said Alicia.

So they found themselves, the next day, on the road to Rome. They had booked an expensive apartment: Alicia was becoming accustomed to the casual laying out of large sums of money. The apartment was fabulous, full of paintings and medieval carvings, with two tiled bathrooms and an enormous drawing room. It was only a stone's throw away from the Colosseum. On their first evening they strolled around the streets hand in hand, stopping to eat at a small, exclusive restaurant. Chris drank bottled water.

They spent the next day touring the Roman ruins. Now they were completely on their own Alicia found she could sometimes forget about Chris's background. They'd more things in common than either of them had suspected—an interest in archaeology for one. Chris spoke Italian reasonably well and took charge of communication with the locals and ordering their meals. Alicia even broached the subject of the thieving and bad behaviour, without mentioning Henry. Chris had the good grace to look embarrassed and said: "I suppose it's some kind of hangover from school. I could try to rein it in a bit."

That night in the apartment it grew icily cold. Alicia awoke with a start—she got up carefully so as not to wake Chris. In the drawing room the moonlight shone through the window and made shadows grow out of the carved wooden angels on the wall. She could feel the pull of the night outside, the still noisy streets, the clubs open till dawn. She went to the window and the woman in the old-fashioned dress was there, waving at her, beckoning her to come out. Back in the bedroom was Chris, tee-total and shorn of bad behaviour, his trust fund safe and a lucrative career in the offing. And if not Chris, there was Henry. Alicia dressed quickly and went out into the night.

War Games

Lucy was an awkward child, unlike Oliver and Sam who, when it was dry, played outside most of the time. She spent a great deal of the summer holiday visiting the library, reading in her room and researching online. It was difficult to persuade her to go out in the garden, and she refused point blank to play with her younger brothers, or any of the girls of her own age who lived nearby. She was the kind of child who asked a lot of questions and didn't always wait for the answers.

As the holiday progressed the weather grew hotter. Lucy spent more and more time in her room hogging the electric fan, reading about some of the many things that interested her. Thirsty for arcane knowledge, she had borrowed a book about "real" hauntings from the library, fuelling her growing enthusiasm for the supernatural. This had supplanted her fascination with evolution and string theory.

"Shouldn't we have a ghost?" Lucy asked her mother. "This is an old house so surely there should be one."

Alison Marchmount sighed. "I've never had the slightest inkling that there is anything spooky here, so there's no need for you to worry."

"I'm not worried. I *want* to see a ghost."

"Well, it's not going to happen," said Alison firmly.

Unbeknownst to her parents Lucy began setting her alarm to go off in the middle of the night. She walked quietly into each room with her camera phone. Because the house was old and constructed of many timbers, it contracted as the heat of the day diminished. Lucy recorded the resultant creaks, almost convincing herself that they were the sound of footsteps in the attic. One night, her father caught her wandering about the house and confiscated her alarm clock and phone, putting paid to her nocturnal adventures for a while.

Sam and Oliver spent most of the summer in the garden playing a complicated game called "chase the soldier". There were many rules which changed often, but the game always involved a great deal of fighting and shooting with gun-shaped sticks (Alison refused to buy them toy guns), and grenade-sized pine cones. The shrubbery stood in for the rain forest while the sandpit was the desert. The boys were not interested in Lucy's latest obsession: when they thought about her at all, they regarded her as a member of an alien species.

Now the boys were more independent and at school, Alison was thinking about finding a part time job. She had a degree in history but might as well have left school at sixteen for all the use it had been. The problem was Lucy. Jason said Lucy would grow out of it—whatever "it" was—but Alison was not so sure. She suspected that Lucy had real problems, and going out to work might take her away from her daughter at a difficult age. It was hard to see how she was going to make it work. There was also the small matter of, after twelve years at home, finding someone who might want to employ her.

Jason Marchmount usually came home late. He commuted to London, and when there was a flap on at the bank (there always seemed to be a flap on at the bank), he came back even later. He had dinner with Alison—the children ate earlier—drank some whisky and went to bed. At weekends the family often went on outings, and if Jason was feeling really brave he left his mobile phone at home. He called it "Going Solo".

This weekend it was Lucy's turn to choose the outing. After some research she announced that she would like to go to Chilton Castle, about twenty-five miles to the west of the town where they lived. Despite its proximity, they had not visited the castle before. On Saturday morning Alison programmed the post code into the sat nav, then turned round to Lucy.

"It's not haunted is it?"

Lucy looked sheepish. "Some people say there is a ghost. You can choose whether or not to believe them."

"Try me."

"Well, there's supposed to be a medieval soldier who runs around the battlements with a sword."

"I'd quite like to see a ghost," said Jason.

The boys were intrigued.

"Are there soldiers at the castle?" asked Oliver.

"Not anymore," said Lucy. "But there used to be. Don't you know anything about castles?"

"No," said Sam, "but this outing sounds more interesting than it did five minutes ago."

Lucy insisted on buying a guide book "so we can do it properly".

There was not much left of the castle, just some of the later ancillary buildings and a section of the keep and perimeter wall. It made up for this lack of superstructure with a plethora of information boards. According to these and the guide book the castle had been blasted to pieces during the civil war, then robbed of building stone by the villagers. Sam and Oliver ran around what little there was of it, looking for non-existent soldiers. It was all slightly disappointing, and before long they repaired to the café for cakes and cups of tea.

"Can we go home now?" asked Sam.

"We might as well," said Alison.

Lucy sulked in the car. When they got home she spent most of the rest of the afternoon in her room.

Sam and Oliver went out to the garden and worked on their game. It was now called "medieval soldier". They had looked in the castle guidebook and settled on an illustration which showed an artist's impression of the ghost—a soldier with chain mail, a simple iron helmet and a long sword. In the game they were chased by the medieval soldier around the shed (representing the castle) at the bottom of the garden. They wore their Christmas jumpers in lieu of chain mail, although this meant they quickly overheated. Alison could hear the battle cries from the kitchen and was reassured that they had not wandered out into the road.

After checking his texts and emails, Jason went to sleep on the sofa. The television was switched on—he found it hard to sleep without the radio or television being left on through the night. Alison put a blanket over him and went to the kitchen to make a chocolate cake.

Lucy appeared just as Alison was putting the cake in the oven. Alison offered her the bowl the mixture had been made in, but Lucy shook her head—such childish things were behind her.

"I've been reading about poltergeists," she said.

"What exactly have you been reading?" asked Alison, running hot water into the washing up bowl.

"Just some stuff," said Lucy vaguely.

"You know that ninety per cent of what you find online about that sort of thing is rubbish."

"I think I can tell what's rubbish and what isn't," said Lucy. "This article says that poltergeists are often associated with houses that contain disturbed young girls. Do you think I'm disturbed enough to attract a poltergeist?"

"Lucy, you're not disturbed, you're just a little . . . odd sometimes. And anyway, we don't have a poltergeist, which means you can't be disturbed."

"So you believe the article too!"

"I didn't say that . . . "

Out in the garden the boys had been forced to take off their jumpers and were lying next to the pond, breathing heavily.

"Do you think medieval soldiers stopped for a lie down?"

Oliver laughed. "I doubt it. They'd have lost the battle if they did."

"I like 'medieval soldier' better than 'chase the soldier', don't you?"

"Swords are more fun than guns, even if it is harder to kill someone." Oliver swished his stick in the air.

"Are you ready to play again?" asked Sam.

They stood up and resumed the chase around the shed, running faster and faster until everything blurred around them.

Jason woke suddenly. The news was just finishing, which meant that it would soon be time for dinner. He had meant to go out in the garden and weed for an hour or so, but it was too late for that now. A light rain had begun to fall and the wind was getting up. The rain pattered against the French window. The boys seemed to be still outside so Jason went to call them in.

It was quiet in the garden; there was only the sound of the occasional car on the road. No war whoops or blood curdling cries.

Jason shouted, "It's nearly time for dinner. Come in and wash your hands."

There was only silence.

"Don't make me come and get you!"

He searched the shrubbery, then behind the shed. There were two discarded jumpers by the pond. He picked them up and folded them over his arm.

"Sam, Oliver, I'm not going to play hide-and-seek. Come out from wherever you are. Mum will have dinner ready any minute."

He looked over the hedge and up and down the road, then he opened up the shed. There were only cobwebs, tins of old paint, a lawn mower and deck chairs. He searched again through the shrubbery. There was no trace of them. The first waves of panic washed through him.

After the police had gone, Alison made Jason and Lucy sit down and eat cold pizza and chocolate cake. None of them were hungry. Jason went out with their neighbours Bill and Leon to look for Oliver and Sam. The police sergeant said that the boys were probably hiding somewhere or playing with other children. There would be a house-to-house search of the area. Alison and Lucy stayed at home in case there was any news: according to the sergeant it was most likely that the boys would come home of their own accord.

Alison told Sergeant Clifton that Sam and Oliver had never wandered off before, even though they had briefly run away when the family were on holiday in Spain. They had come back before anyone missed them, which was shameful enough in itself. Alison felt light-headed, and her heart fluttered like a bird in a cage. Scenarios of what might be happening to the boys came unbidden into her mind. She wished now that she had gone out hunting for them with Jason. It would've been better than staying at home with nothing to do but worry.

Lucy was puzzled by the boys running away. They had such a good set up at home it seemed a daft thing to do. She was not unduly worried because she knew they were resourceful and could look after themselves, even though they were only nine and seven. Lucy had never run away from home because she couldn't think of anywhere to go, although there had been times when it seemed like a good idea.

"Don't worry, Mum. They'll be okay."

"They'll be hungry now. Oh, where are they, Lucy? I think my heart will break."

❧

The time dragged interminably. Then, just before midnight, when they were giving up hope of the boys being found quickly, Jason burst in carrying Oliver.

"Call an ambulance!"

Alison dived for the phone.

Leon came in with Sam over his shoulder. "They're breathing, but we can't get them to wake up."

They laid the boys on the floor and Leon, who had taken a first aid course at work, put them into the recovery position. Alison fetched a duvet and placed it over them. They felt very cold.

"Where did you find them?" asked Alison, who didn't know whether to laugh or cry.

"They were under the shed," replied Jason.

"What were they doing there?"

"I don't expect we'll find out until they wake up."

The ambulance took three quarters of an hour to reach them, and the boys were still unconscious when it arrived. A paramedic checked them over but couldn't find any head traumas, bruising or wounds.

"It's a mystery," she said. "Leave them where they are and talk to them. Eventually they'll come round. In the meantime, call your doctor if you have any concerns."

Alison asked Lucy to talk to the boys. Although she felt self-conscious at first, she was soon telling them about her researches into ghosts and the supernatural, about Borley Rectory and the Society for Psychical Research, about poltergeists and legends of huge black dogs which roamed the countryside. She stroked their faces, poked them and called them by their names. There was not a flicker of consciousness from either of them.

Alison could stand it no longer. She threw several glasses of ice cold water over their faces. There was some spluttering and then they both sat up. Alison burst into tears.

"What were you doing under the shed?" Lucy asked.

Oliver rubbed his eyes. "It's not a shed, it's a castle. We were hiding from the soldier."

"They were playing one of their games," said Lucy.

"Which game?" Jason asked.

"It's a new one," said Sam, "but we didn't think it would be so real."

Oliver sobbed, "We had to hide under the shed, he was coming at us with his sword."

"The children in this house have far too much imagination," grumbled Jason, looking at Alison.

"I don't know why you're looking at me," she said.

After she had made the boys warm milky drinks and sandwiches Alison put them to bed. Lucy went back up to her room and researched medieval soldiers until Jason came in and told her to go to sleep.

In the morning the boys were still groggy. Alison made them sit on the sofa with a duvet over them and brought them their breakfast on trays. Lucy sat in her father's arm chair (Jason had gone to thank Leon and Bill for helping with the search).

"How come *you* got to see the ghost?" she asked.

"We didn't," said Sam. "The soldier was real."

"His sword was sharp, we watched him hack through the shrubbery," said Oliver.

"How could he have been a real person? Unless someone dressed up as a medieval soldier and chased you round the shed."

"I don't know," said Oliver miserably. "All I know is that he *seemed* real. First we were on our own, and then he was there."

"Mum says there are no such things as ghosts, but there's been a lot of research and I believe in them. He must've been the ghost from the castle."

"I suppose it would be quite cool to have seen one," said Sam uncertainly

"No one will believe us," said Oliver.

"We don't have to tell anyone," said Lucy.

Lucy woke in the middle of the night and got out of bed. Because it had been such a humid day the house creaked even more than usual. She crept into each room, hopeful that there would be something to see. The streetlight outside bathed the interior in an orange glow. She looked out of the French windows at the garden, willing the soldier to appear, but there was nothing there except the shrubs swaying in the breeze. Pulling the blanket over her she lay down on the sofa, intending to wait out the night, but after only a few minutes she fell asleep.

Jason found Lucy on the sofa the next morning when he got up for work.

"You'd better go back to bed before your mother catches you."

After her nocturnal wanderings Lucy felt tired, and instead of reading in her room she spent the morning hanging around her mother.

"Do you believe in heaven, Mum? I think I do, but I don't know where ghosts fit in. Perhaps they're in Purgatory, or somewhere else in between."

"Do animals go to heaven? I think they do."

"Is it only intelligent people who believe in ghosts? Lots of famous Victorians did. It means I must be intelligent, don't you think?"

Alison, who was stripping the beds, found it hard to be patient with Lucy. As well as doing the housework, she was trying to keep an eye on Sam and Oliver, who were in the living room playing a car racing game. They were not allowed in the garden.

Boredom forced Lucy outside. She fetched the torch from the kitchen and shone it under the shed. There was nothing to see except some anaemic weeds and an old tennis ball. The shrubbery had indeed been hacked about, but it could have been done by the boys with their sticks. It seemed wrong that Oliver and Sam had conjured up a ghost when she was the one with the real interest in the supernatural. When she grew up, she decided, she would become a famous ghost hunter and prove to the world that ghosts really existed. Lucy went back inside and up to her room.

Oliver and Sam were tiring of their car racing game. The sun was shining and it seemed wrong that they were indoors. It was a waste of a nice day. From the French windows they could see the shrubbery and beyond it the shed. Memories of the scary parts of their adventure were fading fast.

"Do you think Mum would mind if we went out for a minute?"

"She's upstairs with Lucy, so she won't know."

Sam slid open the French window. Bird song flooded the room.

"We could play 'chase the soldier'."

"Let's not go near the shed though."

"Okay. We'll have to be quiet."

The boys raced out into the sunshine.

Alison persuaded Lucy to help her put clean sheets on the beds—it was rare for Lucy to assist with anything. They carried the dirty bedding down to the utility room and stuffed some of it into the washing machine. Alison made a cup of tea and drank it at the kitchen table.

"Don't you think there should be more government research into the supernatural? Maybe there already is and they keep it secret. I'd like to work in that department. I wonder what qualifications I'd need."

"I thought you wanted to be a scientist."

"If I could scientifically prove ghosts exist then there would be no doubt about it."

When Alison went to check on the boys she was horrified to find the French window open and the room empty. She felt sick as she ran out into the garden.

"Sam! Oliver!"

Lucy helped her search the shed and the shrubbery, but there was no sign of them.

"Not again!" wailed Alison.

When she had finished ringing round the neighbours, she phoned Jason at work.

"I'll come home as soon as I can," he said. "Where have the little blighters got to now? You'd better phone the police."

Sergeant Clifton seemed more suspicious this time, and asked if everything was all right at home. Alison said: "Of course things aren't right, our sons keep disappearing."

Lucy felt it was time for an explanation.

"They're probably with the ghost of the medieval soldier. He seems to have followed us home from Chilton Castle and he's been chasing the boys. I don't think he's particularly friendly, so there's good reason to be worried about them."

There was a short silence, then Alison said: "You'll have to excuse my daughter. The boys have been playing war games in the garden, that's all."

The sergeant was writing in his notebook. He glanced up at Lucy.

"If you have anything more to tell me, you'd better come out with it now."

"They might be at the castle," she said. The sergeant gave her a hard stare.

The house to house search threw up no trace of the boys. Alison phoned all the local hospitals and anyone else she could think of. In the end, as a last resort, Sergeant Clifton drove out to Chilton Castle in the patrol car. He decided that Lucy knew more about the disappearance than she was admitting.

It wasn't long before he found the boys inside the keep, curled up together like sleeping puppies. He had to shake them hard to wake them. Neither of the boys appeared to have any idea where they were or how they had got there.

"The medieval soldier was in the shrubbery," said Oliver.

"He was very angry," said Sam. "He tripped Oliver up and pinned him to the ground. I hit him on his helmet with a stone but it didn't stop him. He spun round and pushed me over."

"Then you were shaking us awake."

The sergeant helped the boys into the back of his patrol car and drove them home. Alison, although relieved, was also furious.

"I've told you never to accept lifts from strangers. How could you be so stupid?"

"But, Mummy," sobbed Sam, "we didn't."

Sergeant Clifton explained. "They say they can't remember anything." He stared at Lucy. "We'll be looking into how they got to the castle."

Lucy frowned, "I told you, it was the soldier. They were his prisoners and he took them back to his base."

When Jason got home he sent Lucy to her room and gave the boys a good talking to.

"We'll have to have an exorcism," said Lucy on her way out. "Or some kind of ceremony. It's the only way to get rid of him. I wish I could see him before he goes, though. He seems to be very angry about something. Maybe I could talk him round."

Alison and Jason held crisis talks in the kitchen. They couldn't shut the boys indoors for ever, and were equally worried about Lucy, who seemed to be disappearing into a haze of irrational beliefs.

"Maybe we should go on holiday," said Alison suddenly.

"It would certainly take us away from the problem," mused Jason. "I'm sure I could talk my way into a few days' leave."

They hired a holiday cottage near Weymouth from a friend and within a few days were on their way down to Dorset in the car. Lucy was sulking—she wanted to stay at home. Jason had forbidden her to bring her computer and was himself "Going Solo", having left his mobile phone in his desk drawer. The boys had their faces glued to the window. The good weather continued and holiday traffic clogged the roads.

The cottage was smaller than it looked online, but it had a big garden and a living room which accommodated them all. Alison rustled up some food and opened a bottle of wine. After dinner Lucy took a book up to her new bedroom, which was bigger than her room at home. Oliver and Sam had bunk beds in a bedroom at the other end of the landing. Alison was aghast that there was only one bathroom for the whole family.

Alison put the boys to bed and joined Jason in another glass of wine. Although it was still the height of summer the little cottage with its thick walls felt damp and chilly. Jason lit the fire and put on some coal from the scuttle. Soon the flames licked up the chimney and the room began to feel more comfortable. For the first time in days they felt they could relax.

"We'll let Lucy read for a bit longer," said Jason.

"You mustn't spoil her," said Alison.

Jason stretched out his legs. "This is the life. No phones, no computers. It could be thirty years ago."

"No shop, no buses, and no pub," said Alison. "This village is definitely twenty-first century."

"Let's go out somewhere tomorrow. Just get in the car and drive. It'd be like the old days before the children came along."

Alison smiled. "Okay. We'll do it."

It was drizzling in the morning. Jason found some board games in a cupboard and they spent several hours playing scrabble and draughts. Lucy soon found joining in tiresome and fetched her book from the bedroom. She had brought a pile of books from the library; this one was about extra sensory perception and remote viewing. After lunch the rain stopped and the sun came out. Lucy would far rather have spent the afternoon in the cottage reading but Jason and Alison would not leave her on her own, so she had to get in the back of the car with the boys for what her parents described as "a jaunt". Jason backed out of the drive and headed north.

"Come on, Lucy," said Jason. "Live dangerously. You need to get out of the house once in a while and engage with the real world."

"I don't see why," said Lucy. "I was having an adventure of the mind."

Oliver and Sam were fighting over a bottle of water.

They stopped at a supermarket on the outskirts of Dorchester, where Alison shopped while the others waited in the car. The boys argued about football teams. Lucy stared out of the window at the people unloading their shopping from trolleys.

"This isn't much of a jaunt," she said.

"Give it time," said Jason.

They continued on until they reached Sherborne, where they stopped for a cup of coffee. Bored and fractious, the boys behaved badly in the café, talking at the top of their voices and swinging on the chairs. Jason and Alison were at a loss to know what to do with them.

"I know," said Lucy, "let's go to Maiden Castle."

Alison looked at her in horror.

"It's not *that* kind of castle, it's a prehistoric hillfort near Dorchester. The boys could run around there. It's massive."

For want of any better ideas Jason and Alison agreed, and they drove south again.

It was quite a walk from the car park to the hillfort's elaborate Iron Age entrance, a complicated arrangement of curvilinear banks and ditches which had been constructed to protect the fort from tribal enemies and the incursions of the Romans. There were even false entrances, and more than once the Marchmounts became lost in the prehistoric maze. The sun beat down and Alison began to feel sick and disorientated. The children were strangely quiet and even Jason had stopped chivvying them along.

At last they found their way into the interior of the fort. To their surprise it was crowded with people. A battle re-enactment event seemed to be in progress, even though they could see few other tourists around. Two armies were ranged on either side of the grassy interior of the fort, and camps had been set up, with tents, cooking fires and camp followers. The smell of wood smoke permeated the air. Most of the participants were dressed as soldiers, with replica swords and shields. They seemed to be lined up waiting for battle to commence.

"Soldiers," said Oliver, his eyes wide. "Hundreds of them."

Alison felt queasy. "I'm not sure we should stay."

Jason took out his camera. "I need a picture of this!"

As the camera clicked there was a loud cry. One of the soldiers peeled off and ran towards them—he was holding a long sword. Oliver and Sam yelled in fright as the soldier drew closer: Alison and Jason froze. The sword glinted in the sun as the soldier shifted its weight in his hands and renewed his charge at the boys.

He was only a few metres away when Lucy stepped in front of her brothers. A look of horror came over the soldier's face, but he could not stop in time. As his sword sliced into Lucy he fell to his knees. Lucy lay on the ground, blood gushing from the wound in her side. The soldier groaned and picked her up, cradling her in his arms. Sam was sure he saw Lucy smile, or maybe it was a grimace of pain.

Later, Alison and Jason attempted to explain to a dubious police officer how, one minute the soldier and Lucy were locked in a bloody embrace, the next they had disappeared into thin air.

The Attempt

Saskia could see that the ice near the shore was several centimetres thick. Pieter had told her that the lake never froze over entirely, that there was always an expanse of water at the centre which remained liquid. As he had also insisted that there were monsters in the bottom of the lake, she thought it was probably safe not to believe him.

She stepped tentatively onto the ice, her booted feet sliding a little on the slippery surface. The lake was so large that it was impossible for her to see to its centre. Ahead was a vast expanse of white. Pieter had been taken into the city for his piano lesson so she should have at least three hours, more than enough time for her attempt. It was not fair that Pieter should have the piano lessons that she wanted so badly, just because he was two years older. He wasn't even particularly enthusiastic about them, but whining and arguing for lessons had so far got her nowhere.

Pieter said that no one had ever walked across the frozen lake, that if she did then it would be a world record. Saskia was not sure if she believed him about the world record but it sounded exciting. She picked up her pace over the ice, heading towards where she thought the middle of the lake must be. It was a beautifully still, bitterly cold day—her padded coat, hat and gloves kept out the worst of the chill—the sky was a translucent pale blue. After three or four minutes she turned and looked back to the shore. The buildings were far away already, small, like the toy town she and Pieter had created from their plastic building blocks, populated by tiny articulated figures. She thought she could just make out their house up on the rise, bigger than its neighbours, the red paint standing out from the ochre and yellow all around. The cold seemed to be keeping everyone inside.

Saskia marched on over the ice. When she turned round again, the houses were just specks of colour. All around her was a dull expanse of white, and Saskia began to be uncertain of which direction she should take. According to Pieter the other side of the lake was another country, so she would, strictly speaking, need a passport, but he said that the people of the country would be glad to see her so it wouldn't matter that she didn't have one. He said they would help celebrate her world record. Saskia had never been abroad and this was one of the great attractions of the attempt. Apart from showing Pieter that she could do it. She picked a spot on the horizon and headed for it.

There were bubbles of air trapped beneath the ice that expanded and contracted under the pressure of her feet. Saskia grew so entranced with watching them that she lost contact with her spot on the horizon. Still, it did not matter, as long as she was aiming in more or less the right direction. The far shore might be as wide as the one she had started from, so exactly where she landed was not important, as long as it was inhabited.

After an hour or so Saskia felt thirsty. Feeling proud of her forethought, she took out a small bottle of water from her coat pocket. After a couple of sips, she put the bottle back and extracted a chocolate bar. She ate a few squares, then wrapped up the remainder carefully. An icy breeze was now blowing from the far shore and the sky had clouded over. Saskia shivered. The town was no longer visible behind her, and she could see nothing ahead but ice.

As she strode on over the lake, Saskia thought of the little figures in the toy town back home. Her favourite was a family called Petrov, with two children, a boy and a girl. She and Pieter put them through all kinds of adventures and traumatic experiences, including a fire and an earthquake. The boy, Boris, was the hero of most of these escapades, the girl, Anna, the coper, the nurse, the cook. Saskia liked her practical strength. Pieter often pretended that he didn't really care about the Petrovs and their adventures, but he spent as much time as Saskia thinking up scenarios and acting them out. The senior Petrovs were distant figures, often away at work or outside gardening. One of the best things about the toy town was that Boris and Anna did not have to go to school.

Saskia stopped and shielded her eyes. Ahead, in the far distance, tiny black specks were appearing. She walked on at a faster pace. Her watch told her that she had been walking for an hour and a half, and although she was beginning to feel tired, she was glad that she would reach the far shore at her first attempt.

As Saskia drew closer, the wooden buildings took shape. They were dowdier than those of her own town, being mostly unpainted log cabins. There were no people to be seen. She stepped off the ice onto the frozen ground and approached the largest cabin, but when she knocked on the door, no one answered. She tried some of the other cabins, returning at last to the largest. Carefully she opened the door. Inside there were items of furniture covered in dust, a cooker and an iron bedstead. It looked as if it was a summer house that no one had visited for a long time.

Feeling somewhat crestfallen that there was no one to help her celebrate, Saskia resolved to make her way around the shore until she found an inhabited settlement. After walking for another half an hour, she realised that it was taking too long. She would not now be able to get home in time to greet Pieter and their parents on their return from the city. Indeed she would be in trouble for staying out on her own. She wished that she had left a note saying that she had gone to Maria's house.

Saskia stepped onto the ice and headed back towards the centre of the lake. After an hours' walk, although she scanned the horizon carefully, there was no trace of the cheerful colours of her town, just the endless white of the ice. Saskia drank the rest of the water from the bottle and ate all the chocolate. She was beginning to feel cold. In a few hours it would be dark.

How would she prove to Pieter that she had really walked over the lake to the far shore? She kicked herself that she hadn't brought some artefact from the cabin to show him. She could imagine his scornful face as she pleaded with him to believe her. Then she realised that even if she brought evidence he might still decide she was being untruthful. Hot shameful tears trickled down her cheeks.

Saskia was trying not to panic, but it felt as if the ice stretched on for ever. When she thought it through, she realised that it was possible that she had not reached the far shore at all, but had instead cut across a segment of the lake. That would explain why it was now taking so much longer to get home—she was walking across the lake's true diameter, which would be much further than her outward journey. In any case she was lost, and there was nothing she could do except keep on walking.

After another hour, Saskia stopped and again scanned the horizon. This time she thought she could see some specks which might be buildings. After another half an hour she could see definite blocks of colour. As she drew nearer, she realised that it was not her home town but another with a more regular layout. The houses were rectangular and built of primary coloured bricks, with flat roofs. Each house had a square of green lawn and a tarmac drive. Saskia stepped off the ice and onto the land. The town seemed familiar although she was sure she had never been there before. She headed for a prominent red house and knocked on the door. It was answered by a man in a V-necked jumper and tie.

"Hello," he said. "You look exhausted."

Saskia stumbled into the kitchen. "I'm sorry to bother you but I've walked across the lake and now I'm lost."

A woman in a flowered dress came into the kitchen. She switched on the kettle.

"I'll make you a hot drink and you can have some toast and honey," she said. "You'll feel better when you have something inside you."

The man looked down at her. "You're rather young to be out on your own. Don't worry though, we'll look after you."

The woman spooned hot chocolate powder into a mug. The kettle boiled and she poured in the hot water. Two slices of bread were placed in the toaster. "Take off your coat and boots, it's quite warm in here," she said.

Saskia did as she was told, then sipped the delicious hot chocolate. Soon she was gobbling the toast and honey. After she had finished she felt sleepy. The woman took her into the living room and encouraged her to lie down on the sofa. It wasn't long before Saskia had fallen into a dreamless sleep.

When she awoke it was dark outside and the curtains had been drawn. The room was very warm, warmer than the living room in her own house. She saw that two almost grown up children were sitting on the floor, reading books. As she sat up they turned to face her.

"Hello Saskia," said the boy. "Do you know who we are?"

"Yes," said Saskia, "you're Boris and Anna."

Anna laughed. "You see, Boris, I told you she would know."

Boris Petrov stood up. "Our parents are looking after you. They say you walked across the lake. No-one has crossed the lake on foot before. There are signs everywhere warning people not to walk on the ice."

"I was perfectly safe. I am quite small and the ice was thick enough to take my weight."

"It was very brave of you," said Anna. "Father said you were tired and cold when you got here."

"I feel better now I have slept a little," said Saskia defensively. "Pieter said I would set a world record if I crossed the lake and as I am the first person to do so then he must be right."

"Congratulations," said Boris.

At that moment Mrs. Petrova came in carrying three glasses of lemonade on a tray. "This is to help celebrate your great achievement," she said, handing them round to the children. "The lake does not freeze over completely every year, so you have been lucky that you chose to make your attempt during an exceptionally cold spell."

Boris raised his glass: "To Saskia."

Saskia gulped down the fizzy drink. Mrs. Petrova looked at the clock on the mantelpiece. "It is quite late and time for Boris and Anna to go to bed. I suggest that you should sleep again, Saskia."

Saskia suddenly gasped in dismay—"But my parents, and Pieter! They will be wondering where I am!"

"We will worry about that in the morning," said Mrs. Petrova.

Saskia sank down on the sofa under the blanket and to her surprise did not wake up until half way through the next morning. She found the Petrovas in the kitchen having a late breakfast.

"Can I telephone my parents, please?"

Mr. Petrov cleared his throat. "I am afraid we're so remote and insignificant that we have not been considered for telephones," he said. "The best thing is if you stay with us until Pieter realises that you are here. Don't worry. We will make sure you have enough food. You can have a bath now if you would like one."

"But I don't understand. How will Pieter know that I am here?"

"He will work it out," said Anna.

"Perhaps he will think to provide us with a telephone and then our problem will be solved," said Boris.

After her bath Saskia played board games with Boris and Anna, but her mind was elsewhere.

"I think I should leave now and try to find my way home," she said. "My parents may have called the police."

"Oh, I shouldn't worry," said Boris. "Pieter will cover for you. He will think up some reason why you are not there."

Anna smiled encouragingly. "And you are not fully recovered from your exertions of yesterday."

After lunch there was a knock at the door. To Saskia's amazement, Mrs. Petrova showed Pieter into the living room.

"Hello, little sis!" he said cheerfully. "So you're saying you made it to the far shore?"

"I'm not just saying it, I did it!" Saskia replied crossly. "I knew you wouldn't believe me."

"Whatever," said Pieter. "*If* you say so. Only you can know. I hope you've been making notes about anything we need to provide here. A telephone is the most obvious thing. Mr. Petrov is quite cross about that."

"They don't have a television or computers."

"No. I suppose we envisaged them existing in an earlier time. A time before those things were commonplace."

"You're pretty inconsistent about the things you have provided," said Boris. "We have a toaster but no television. I, for one, would appreciate being able to communicate with the outside world."

Anna nodded. "It would help make the down times less boring."

"Down times?" queried Saskia.

"You know," said Pieter, "when we're not playing with them."

"Where do our parents think I am?" Saskia asked Pieter.

"I told them you said you were staying the night with Maria. I've come to collect you and take you home."

"You are welcome to stay as long as you like," said Anna, politely.

"We'd better not cross the boundary for long," said Pieter. "Otherwise we may never get back."

Saskia put on her coat, hat and gloves, and after thanking Mr. and Mrs. Petrov, she and Pieter let themselves out of the front door. It was a cold, grey day. Pieter took Saskia's hand and led her to the edge of the ice.

"We needn't walk on the lake, we can just follow the shore. It is more dangerous walking on ice, especially with two of us."

"How was your piano lesson?" asked Saskia.

"Okay, I suppose. To tell you the truth I'm getting a bit bored of the piano. I've asked Mum if I can have guitar lessons instead. She said you can take over the piano lessons if you like."

Saskia whooped for joy. "How far do we have to walk to get home?" she asked.

"I don't know," said Pieter. "It took about an hour for me to get here, but then I walked over the lake."

"I really did walk across from the far shore, Pieter."

"Well then," he said, "it's something that you'll never need to do again."

Breath of Life

After wandering around the car boot sale in the rain for half the morning, Tilda was ready to buy almost anything. Besides, the dummy made her laugh. He was handsome and bald, with articulated arms and legs, dressed in a soggy tweed suit which probably dated to the 1960s. His feet were bare. She haggled over the price, as you were meant to, then carried him (Cassy and Linda screaming with laughter) to Cassy's car. He sat in the back next to Tilda until they were dropped off at Tilda's flat in Eastbourne, the other two travelling on to Brighton.

He was surprisingly heavy, considering he was made of plastic, his eyes and lips a pale fawn, like the rest of him. Tilda dragged him up the stairs, unlocked the door, carried him into her bedroom and sat him in the chair on which she usually laid her clothes. She took off her coat and hung it on the hook on the back of the door.

"Well, Handsome, welcome to your new home. I hope you'll find it comfortable."

The joke was in danger of wearing thin now Cassy and Linda had gone.

She moved him to the kitchen where he sat while she made a casserole for Sunday lunch.

"I don't know why I bother cooking fancy meals just for me, but my mother would have approved. Do you think we all turn into our mothers, Handsome?"

The dummy smiled his bland smile; the corners of his long mouth turned faintly upwards. Tilda ate her meal in the kitchen. After she had washed up she watched a film on television. She sat the dummy next to her on the sofa, his hand resting on her knee. Tilda laid her head on his shoulder and he slid sideways, his downward trajectory halted by the armrest.

Later that evening, in her bedroom, she felt strangely coy getting undressed in front of him. While she lay in bed he sat in his suit on her bedroom chair. She thought she would buy him some more clothes so that he did not look so uncomfortable, dressed as he was for a grouse shoot, or a country walk.

In the morning Tilda sat him in the kitchen and ate her breakfast. She cleared her throat.

"I have to go to work this morning, Handsome. You can read a book or something while I'm gone. In fact, I'll leave you next to the living room window so you can watch the world go by."

During her lunch break Tilda visited several charity shops, buying clothes for the dummy. Back at the flat she took off his tweed suit, exposing his slim, sexless body, and dressed him in a navy tracksuit. She had also bought a powder blue dressing gown and some slippers. They sat together on the sofa in front of a gritty police drama, Tilda watching the more gruesome scenes from behind the dummy's shoulder.

"You have nerves of steel, Handsome."

On Friday Cassy and Linda drove over for a take-away meal and a drink. In fact there was a great deal of drinking, and Handsome ended up naked, sprawled on the living room floor.

"He's almost perfect," said Linda.

"Almost," said Cassy.

"He's a good listener," said Tilda. "Aren't you, Handsome?"

Late the next morning, after the girls and their hangovers had left, Tilda sat him in an armchair and pulled his tracksuit back on.

"I'm sorry," she whispered guiltily. "I won't let that happen again," and, patting his hand, she leaned over and kissed him gently on the lips.

"No need to be sorry," he said.

Tilda stared at him in astonishment.

"I . . . I . . . only meant we shouldn't have stripped you."

"Oh, I don't mind. Why do you think I was manufactured without genitals? It makes being naked far less embarrassing."

He was speaking, but not moving. Tilda decided that it must be some kind of auditory hallucination brought on by excessive alcohol consumption.

"What should I call you? What's your name?"

"Handsome is as good a name as any," he said. "By the way, these are great clothes for lounging in. And I like the dressing gown and slippers. Do please continue to sit me next to the living room window. It's good to watch the people passing by below. I would wave if I could."

Tilda picked him up and sat him in the chair next to the window. "There you are," she said. She went into the bedroom to think things over.

Later, Tilda put her hand on his shoulder. "I'm going out this afternoon," she said. "I've got a date. His name is Marcus, he's one of the trainee solicitors at work. He's taking me out to Hampden Park for a walk and an ice cream. He likes the sound of his own voice but I think it's because he's nervous. He is quite nice to look at, though not as handsome as you, of course."

She dressed Handsome in his dressing gown and slippers.

"You don't mind me going out with Marcus, do you?"

"Why should I mind? I have a very specific role. I can't take you out and show you a good time now, can I? I will be here in my dressing gown and slippers, waiting for you to come home."

Marcus took Tilda's arm proprietorially almost as soon as they met. The park was full of families and children playing football and feeding the ducks. Marcus talked about work and occasionally remembered to ask Tilda a question about herself. They ate their ice creams by the pond, Tilda trying hard not to spill hers down her blouse. Marcus seemed to be one of those naturally elegant people who did everything well.

Tilda had invited him back to her flat, forgetting for a moment that the dummy was in the living room. As they climbed the stairs she explained to Marcus that she was looking after part of an art installation for a friend. Marcus raised his eyebrows on seeing Handsome sitting in the chair next to the window.

"Doesn't he give you the creeps?"

"I find him rather comforting."

"Well I hope he won't mind if I kiss you?"

Marcus was a good kisser. Soon they were on the sofa, fumbling with each other's clothes.

"Look, Marcus, this is great but . . . "

"Let's go through to the bedroom," he said, "if you're feeling uncomfortable in here."

It seemed churlish to refuse. Afterwards, Marcus got dressed and said he had to read up on a case. He let himself out. Tilda returned to the living room in her dressing gown. She sat down next to the dummy. He was still looking out of the window.

"Are you okay, Handsome?" she asked.

"Why shouldn't I be?" he answered. "After all, I always have a smile on my face. Maybe I should be asking you."

"I don't think there'll be another date, he was far too keen to leave."

"I hope it was nothing to do with me?"

"He barely notices anything apart from himself," said Tilda.

"Do you have any other gentlemen friends?" asked Handsome.

"Not so you'd notice," said Tilda. "Apart from you, of course. I tend towards the one-night stand."

"Ah, the reproductive imperative! I am quite glad to be free of it, although it is fascinating to watch you young people going about your business, hardly aware of what is making you tick."

"Is there not another dummy waiting for you somewhere?"

"Alas, no. We posed in the department store, but only for the customers. It is our role to ape and serve humanity, not to live lives like yours."

"But what about you, Handsome? Aren't you an anomaly?"

"I have a new role, to keep you company and keep you safe. A quid pro quo for you rescuing me from the car boot sale."

Tilda shuddered and reached over and stroked his bald head. "It was horrid, wasn't it?" She picked him up and carried him to the sofa where they sat in silence in each other's arms for some time.

"I don't know what I want," said Tilda at last.

"It is partially out of your hands," said Handsome. "You must simply carry on and await events. One day a young man will see your worth and in turn be worthy of you."

"You old romantic," said Tilda, nuzzling his neck.

"I don't think you're the type to be alone for long, he said. "You're too affectionate."

At work on Monday Marcus ostentatiously avoided Tilda. When she finally caught up with him she whispered, "Don't worry, I haven't told anyone you slept with me."

"I'm not bothered if you have," he said, "I just thought you'd prefer it if I was discreet. I like you, Tilda, and I'd love to go out with you again."

They arranged to meet at an Italian restaurant in town. Tilda spent several hours getting herself ready, pinning up her hair, choosing and ironing a dress.

"Are you sure he's worth it," said Handsome. "I thought he was just a one-night stand."

"Maybe I misjudged him," said Tilda. "He seems to like me, anyway, and that's half the battle."

In the restaurant Marcus took charge, ordering the food and wine. The food was unpretentious and delicious. He had bought her a red rose. They talked about work, although they had agreed not to before the meal. As a legal assistant Tilda was somewhat junior to Marcus, although they were, as it turned out, the same age. After the meal Marcus asked if they could go back to her flat (he shared a house with other students) and Tilda could not think of a good reason to refuse. As she let them into the living room and switched on the light Marcus jumped.

"Oh God, it's that bloody dummy," he said. "You've put him in a dressing gown—how weird is that?"

"It's pretty weird," said Tilda, "but he likes it."

"How can you tell?"

"You can see how comfortable he looks."

"You're a bit odd," said Marcus, "but I like you anyway. Where's this art installation he's a part of?"

"In London," said Tilda vaguely. "I might decide to keep him, though."

"What do you mean?"

"He may not be needed for the installation, in which case he can stay here."

When Marcus had gone Tilda took her cup of coffee into the living room. She squeezed into the chair next to the dummy, who was still looking out of the window into the night.

"How was it?" he asked.

"Fine, thank you, Handsome."

"Do you know I have watched fourteen couples in the street below? And two hen parties and many more single people. Not one person seemed to notice me at the window. I suppose I am in too elevated a position here. Far above their worries and dreams."

"Are you getting bored? Shall I leave the television on for you?"

"No, I do not suffer from boredom. I am designed to stay in one position for a long time."

Tilda rose and lifted him up. "Nevertheless, it'll do you good to have a change of scene." She carried him into the bedroom and put him on the chair. The bed was still unmade from earlier. Tilda slid beneath the duvet.

"Are you sure you want me in here," said Handsome. "It's very late."

"Yes," said Tilda. She switched off the light. "We can talk in the dark."

At work the next day Tilda and Marcus found that most of their colleagues seemed to know that they were dating. It turned out that Dale's sister had seen them together in the restaurant, and Dale had told Christine, who had told everybody else. In some ways it was a relief that they needn't hide it, but it also introduced an element of pressure on a relationship that had hardly begun.

Tilda went to Oxfam at lunchtime and bought three casual shirts, a pair of black jeans and two pairs of pyjamas. In Marks and Spencer she bought three pairs of underpants and three pairs of socks. "They're for when we have company, Handsome," she told him that evening.

"I approve," he said, "they show very good judgement on your part. Especially the underwear."

She dressed him in the jeans and a striped shirt, and sat him at the kitchen table while she ate her dinner.

"Refuelling, I see," he said. "Another imperative I do not share."

"Do you know, I've never felt really hungry," said Tilda.

"I haven't experienced any kind of hunger, but then I don't expend energy."

"Your lips don't move when you speak."

"How is Marcus?"

"He's quite lively, thank you. He's coming round soon." Tilda leaned over and unfastened Handsome's top shirt button. "That's better."

Marcus arrived as Tilda was washing the dishes. He sat down opposite the dummy.

"You've dressed him in new clothes," he said. "Aren't you a bit old for playing with dolls?"

"Evidently not."

"So you're not letting the installation have him."

"I haven't decided yet. I like his company. He has a different outlook on life."

Marcus looked at the dummy and made circular "she's crazy" motions with his fingers. The dummy smiled his enigmatic smile.

When she had finished washing up, Tilda went to pick up the dummy, but Marcus insisted on carrying him through to the living room. He sat him in the armchair, even arranged his legs and arms sympathetically. Then Marcus steered Tilda onto the sofa. He sat with his arm around her shoulders and talked about his law course and how he was saving up for a deposit on a flat.

"You're very lucky to have your own place, Tilda. You and your friend here."

"The flat belongs to my uncle, I rent it from him. Let's watch TV shall we? It's all I'm good for this evening."

Marcus switched on the television and they watched a cooking competition and then the police drama she had watched with Handsome the week before. Marcus was a good deal more squeamish than Handsome, and made sarcastic comments about some of the acting and the script. Tilda glanced over at the dummy but he was staring blandly at the TV screen.

Marcus left when the police drama finished. "Three's a crowd," he said. Tilda brought a glass of water into the living room. The news was on.

"He seems like a reasonable person," said the dummy, "if a little immature."

"He's only twenty-three!"

"Some men are fathers by their early twenties."

Tilda spluttered, "That's not likely to happen to Marcus. Not if I have anything to do with it."

"I think you'd make a very good mother," he said. "You seem the maternal type."

Tilda fetched one of the new pairs of pyjamas. She pulled off his shirt and jeans and underwear. "Perhaps we'd better give you a sponge bath, Handsome, you look a little grubby."

She put him in the bath and soaped him all over, then rinsed him off with the shower attachment. Drying him took some time, and only when she was sure he was completely moisture free did she put on the clean pyjamas, slippers and dressing gown. She sat him on the bedroom chair while she got herself ready for bed.

"I must say I feel marvellous," he said.

"Do you, Handsome? I'm glad."

"The only thing is, I'd be a lot more comfortable if I could lie down."

"Well I can't put you on the floor, so you'd better get into bed with me."

"That would be most gratifying."

Tilda took off his dressing gown and slippers and laid him under the duvet. They talked quietly with the light off until Tilda fell asleep.

Tilda slept through the alarm and barely had time to change Handsome into his tracksuit before she left for work. She sat him in his usual chair next to the window.

During the morning the fire brigade were called to a small fire in a block of flats at the other end of the street. The fire fighters escorted everyone out of the building, then two of them disappeared back inside with fire extinguishers. They emerged a quarter of an hour later carrying several blackened and half-melted plastic kitchen appliances: a toaster, a kettle and a grill.

Once the excitement died down and the firemen had left, there was only the usual ebb and flow of human life. The flat was close to the town centre and many people walked up and down the street each day. There was a party of primary school children which, every week-day morning and afternoon walked past in their green and grey uniforms. Another regular was a man who lived in the ground floor flat opposite, who came out only to do his shopping, lugging back large bags of groceries.

After midday the sun shone in through the window. A pigeon landed on the windowsill, bobbing its head at its reflection in the glass. At a quarter to six Tilda turned the corner into the road, carrying a bag full of shopping. She let herself into the door at the bottom of the building, then climbed the stairs to her second floor flat. She kissed Handsome on his cool cheek.

"Hello, have you had a good day?"

"A very good day, thank you."

"Just an omelette tonight, I thought. Cheese. And a salad."

Tilda went into the bedroom and changed into jeans and a t-shirt. As she carried the dummy into the kitchen he said, "I believe it is recommended that you switch off all your electric appliances at the wall before leaving the house."

"I'm sure you're right, but it's difficult to find the time to do it every day."

"It would be the sensible thing to do."

"I will try to remember, just for you."

The omelette was cooked and eaten, and Tilda switched off the hob at the wall when she had finished.

"You see," he said, "it will soon become second nature."

"What would I do without you, Handsome? Marcus is out drinking with friends tonight, so we'll have the evening to ourselves."

Tilda opened a bottle of wine. She carried Handsome into the living room and sat him on the sofa. They watched a film, which he said he found "very interesting". Tilda drank steadily through the evening until she had got through most of the wine.

"Well, Handsome, what am I going to do with you?"

"What do you mean?"

"I can't keep you a secret for ever. If you're going to continue to talk then sooner or later someone else is bound to find out. If it's not just a figment of my imagination, that is. Have you any idea what a sensation you'd be?"

"I speak only to you."

"Will that always be the case? What about Marcus? What if he moves in?"

"Have you asked him to?"

"No. But I might. In a moment of weakness. Marcus or someone else. You're always encouraging me to follow the reproductive imperative."

"You could take up ventriloquism. Make a fortune."

"You'd be a freak show! I don't think either of us want that. Besides, you're *my* freak." Tilda cuddled up to him.

The doorbell rang. Outside were a drunken Marcus and his friends Richard and Stephen. They pushed past Tilda into the living room. Marcus roared with laughter.

"I thought you'd be with our mutual friend. Look at this! Cosy isn't it?" Marcus sat down next to the dummy and picked up Tilda's glass of wine. "Come on feller, take a sip." He raised the glass up to Handsome's lips and tipped it towards him. The wine dribbled down the dummy's chin and onto his tracksuit top. Richard and Stephen guffawed.

"Leave him alone!" shouted Tilda. Before she could pull Marcus away he put his lips to Handsome's and slurped up some of the wine.

"You're jealous," said Handsome. "Tilda doesn't like it, she has more taste."

Marcus stared. "How did he say that?"

"Say what?" asked Stephen.

"He said I'm jealous!" Marcus pushed the dummy onto the floor.

Tilda crouched down and wiped Handsome's face with a tissue.

"You've hurt him, Marcus! What have you done! Are you all right, Handsome?"

"Yes, I think so."

Marcus laughed hysterically. "His name's Handsome?"

"Handsome is as Handsome does," said Handsome.

"Can't you hear him?" said Marcus to Stephen and Richard. "He's talking." They both shook their heads.

Richard turned to Marcus "I think we better take you home."

"Goodbye, Marcus," said the dummy. "Drink plenty of water."

After they had gone Tilda dressed Handsome in his pyjamas.

"The cat's out of the bag now," she said. "What are we going to do?"

"It will take some thinking about," he said.

Out of the corner of her eye, Tilda could have sworn she saw his lips move.

Acknowledgments

My thanks to the following editors and publishers
for the first appearance of these stories, as follows:

"The Bronze Statuette"
was first published in *Supernatural Tales 29*,
edited by David Longhorn, Autumn 2016.

"The Attempt"
was first published in *Shadows & Tall Trees 7*,
edited by Michael Kelly,
Undertow Publications, 2017.

All other stories are
original to this volume.

About the Author

Rosalie Parker co-runs independent UK publisher Tartarus Press with R. B. Russell. She also writes her own strange short stories, which have appeared in many anthologies and five collections. Rosalie grew up on a small farm in Buckinghamshire and worked as an archaeologist before returning to her first love of books. Based in the Yorkshire Dales since 2000, Rosalie and Ray have a grown-up son, Tim.

SWAN RIVER PRESS

Founded in 2003, Swan River Press is an independent publishing company, based in Dublin, Ireland, dedicated to gothic, supernatural, and fantastic literature. We specialise in limited edition hardbacks, publishing fiction from around the world with an emphasis on Ireland's contributions to the genre.

www.swanriverpress.ie

"While small publishers often produce beautiful books, few can match those from Swan River Press."

– Washington Post

"It [is] often down to small, independent, specialist presses to keep the candle of horror fiction flickering . . . "

– The Irish Times

"Swan River Press—cutting edge of New Gothic."

– Joyce Carol Oates

"The redoubtable Brian J. Showers [keeps] the myriad voices of Irish fantasy alive there in Dublin."

– Alan Moore

YOU'LL KNOW WHEN YOU GET THERE

Lynda E. Rucker

A woman returns home to revisit an encounter with the numinous; couples take up residence in houses full of sinister secrets; a man fleeing a failed marriage discovers something ancient and unknowable in rural Ireland . . .

In her introduction, Lisa Tuttle observes that "certain places are doomed, dangerous in some inexplicable, metaphysical way", and the characters in these stories all seem drawn in their own ways to just such places, whether trying to return home or endeavouring to get as far from life as possible. These nine stories by Shirley Jackson Award winner Lynda E. Rucker tell tales of those lost and searching, often for something they cannot name, and encountering along the way the uncanny embedded in the everyday world.

"Indirection is a special skill and it's one that Lynda E. Rucker uses frequently to emphasise those near indefinable moments of social alienation and paranoia, that you just want to get up and run far, far away from."

– Adam L. G. Nevill

"Lynda is the genuine article—a serious, literary author of 'quiet horror' whose work is disquieting, inspiring, and oddly reassuring. It's good to know that there are writers so gifted working in our genre."

– Supernatural Tales

THE SEA CHANGE
& Other Stories

Helen Grant

In her first collection, award-winning author Helen Grant plumbs the depths of the uncanny: Ten fathoms down, where the light filtering through the salt water turns everything grey-green, something awaits unwary divers. A self-aggrandising art critic travelling in rural Slovakia finds love with a beauty half his age—and pays the price. In a small German town, a nocturnal visitor preys upon children; there is a way to keep it off—but the ritual must be perfect. A rock climber dares to scale a local crag with a diabolical reputation, and makes a shocking discovery at the top. In each of these seven tales, unpleasantries and grotesqueries abound—and Grant reminds us with each one that there can be fates even worse than death.

"A brilliant chronicler of the uncanny as only those who dwell in places of dripping, graylit beauty can be."

– Joyce Carol Oates

"Meticulously written and with carefully calculated chills."

– Black Static

DEATH MAKES STRANGERS OF US ALL

R. B. Russell

At the edges of everyday life, on geographical boundaries and in the margins of society, certainties and realities can wear thin. And if we find ourselves in such occult and outland territory late at night, we might glimpse phenomena out of the corner of our eye that cannot possibly be there. At such times even the past, apparently fixed and unchanging in memories and dreams, cannot be relied upon.

But what happens if we find ourselves passing beyond even these frayed perimeters of life? Can others follow us, or are we on our own? And just where will our final journey take us? How can we perceive or understand the changes that death will bring?

"The disorienting title story of R. B. Russell's superb Death Makes Strangers of Us All takes us into an 'unreal city' straight out of Kafka or Borges."

– Michael Dirda, *Washington Post*

"Once again, R. B. Russell has produced a fine collection of remarkable stories told in a captivating, styling fashion."

– Mario Guslandi